"Thank you so much for watching the kids," she said.

"And for doing all this with them. They've always wanted to decorate outside." *But I could never afford that.*

"Why don't you come and join us? It should be a family fort." His grin set her heart racing again. "You know you want to."

"I need to put the grocery bags away and—" Joy paused, thought a moment. How often did she get a chance to just play with her kids? This was a rare opportunity not to be missed. "Okay, I will. For a few minutes. Then I'll start supper."

"It's already in the slow cooker. Soup." He chuckled at her expression. "I told you I can cook. Don't worry. The kids and I cleaned up our mess."

"It's very kind of you," she began, but he shook his head.

"Come on, before it's too dark to see anything." Then he was gone, rushing out the door as if he *wanted* to help her three fatherless kids build a snow fort on a winter's evening.

Sam Calhoun was like no other man Joy had ever met.

Lois Richer loves traveling, swimming and quilting, but mostly she loves writing stories that show God's boundless love for His precious children. As she says, "His love never changes or gives up. It's always waiting for me. My stories feature imperfect characters learning that love doesn't mean attaining perfection. Love is about keeping on keeping on." You can contact Lois via email, loisricher@gmail.com, or on Facebook (loisricherauthor).

Books by Lois Richer

Love Inspired

The Calhoun Cowboys

Hoping for a Father
Home to Heal
Christmas in a Snowstorm

Rocky Mountain Haven

Meant-to-Be Baby
Mistletoe Twins
Rocky Mountain Daddy
Rocky Mountain Memories

Wranglers Ranch

The Rancher's Family Wish
Her Christmas Family Wish
The Cowboy's Easter Family Wish
The Twins' Family Wish

Visit the Author Profile page at Harlequin.com for more titles.

Christmas in a Snowstorm

Lois Richer

LOVE INSPIRED
INSPIRATIONAL ROMANCE

LOVE INSPIRED®
INSPIRATIONAL ROMANCE

ISBN-13: 978-1-335-48856-5

Christmas in a Snowstorm

Copyright © 2020 by Lois M. Richer

Recycling programs for this product may not exist in your area.

This edition published by arrangement with Harlequin Books S.A.

For questions and comments about the quality of this book, please contact us at CustomerService@Harlequin.com.

Love Inspired
22 Adelaide St. West, 40th Floor
Toronto, Ontario M5H 4E3, Canada
www.Harlequin.com

Printed in U.S.A.

For God so loved the world, that he gave his only begotten Son, that whosoever believeth in him should not perish, but have everlasting life.
—*John* 3:16

This book is dedicated to my sister Darcy, who passed away unexpectedly while I was writing this story. Her many friends called her Mrs. Christmas, perhaps because she so well understood that the reason for the season is love. I miss you, Darc.

Chapter One

Talk about a homecoming!

A blizzard wasn't exactly the welcome Sam Calhoun had expected his hometown of Sunshine, Montana, to offer. And yet, after two months in the Middle East, a part of him reveled in guiding his brand-new SUV through gusts of swirling white flakes and thick drifts now creeping in from the highway's covered shoulder.

Today was just two days after Thanksgiving. Imagine what December would bring.

Wait a minute!

Sam leaned forward and peered through the windshield, trying to locate the flash of red that had caught the corner of his eye a moment ago. There it was again. But *what was* it?

He'd spent his youth driving this road. He knew that lifting his foot from the gas pedal was far safer than touching the brakes, even with four-wheel drive, because under this snow lay that most treacherous driving hazard—black ice. One jerk of the wheel could send him careening into the ditch. Since Sam did *not* intend to spend the rest of the night freezing in his car just a few miles from home, he let his vehicle slow to a crawl.

Suddenly his headlights revealed three kids huddled together in front of an old farmhouse.

"What in the world—"

Sam had returned home with the express goal of not getting involved. It had cost him too deeply, too often. Recently, it had almost cost him his life. But how could he ignore kids in a snowstorm? He couldn't.

"Here I go again, God." He eased onto the shoulder, shifted into Park and vaulted out of his car, praying no one was hurt. "What happened?"

"A tree fell on owa house," a little blonde girl informed him, her face just visible in the hooded circle of a red parka with its hood tied closed under her chin.

She'd hardly finished speaking when a gust of wind ripped around the house and almost knocked the smallest child over. Sam reached out and grasped his jacket to steady him.

"Becca," an older boy's voice chided. "You never say the r's right. Let *me* explain." Huge green eyes met Sam's. "Like she said, a huge tree fell on our house. Our mom made us come out here to wait while she gets some of our stuff. Then we're gonna go to the neighbor's to see if we can stay with them tonight. I'm Josh Grainger. This is my sister, Becca, and that's my little brother, Cris."

"I'm Sam." Suddenly aware that the three were shivering and that their outerwear seemed far too insubstantial to withstand a storm like this, he suggested, "Why don't you get in my car and wait for your mom while I go find her?"

"We're not supposed to go in cars with strangers," Josh said calmly.

"Yes, of course you aren't. Sorry." What to do now? "Can you wait here a few minutes more, till I find your mom? Then I'll be happy to drive you wherever you need to go."

"Okay." Josh nodded as he huddled his siblings closer, his thin face pale in the icy breeze.

"What's your mom's name?" Sam asked as he tugged his gloves out of his pocket.

"Joy," Becca said. "Joy Gwainger." Her cute gap-toothed smile reached in and squeezed Sam's heart.

"Grainger," Josh corrected with an eye roll.

"Got it. Don't move now," Sam ordered. He left them shivering and tramped through big drifts, past a crooked snowman who'd lost his hat, to the darkened front door.

"Joy?" he called. Then, "Joy Grainger!"

No response. Since the door wouldn't open, he walked around the side and gasped at the sight. A yard light illuminated a huge cottonwood tree that had fallen and divided the house. On its way down, the treetop had crushed an old, battered car that was now, Sam guessed, way beyond repair. A gust of snow-filled wind smacked him in the face like a cold shower, bringing reality with it. Those kids needed shelter. Now.

"Joy!"

"Yes?" A woman appeared suddenly, clutching a flashlight in one hand and a battered suitcase in the other. She wore a hat—was that an alligator?

Sam stifled his laughter.

"Go ahead, make fun, but this hat is special. It was my Christmas gift from the kids last year, and it's really warm." She shrugged and gave a quirky grin before demanding, "Who are you?"

"Sam Calhoun. Pleased to meet you." He inclined his head in the direction of his vehicle. "Your kids won't get in my car to keep warm without your say-so, and they need to because they're freezing. You must be, too. Come on, I'll give you a ride to wherever you need to go."

"Calhoun?" she said, eyes narrowing. She stood as if rooted to the spot. "Um, Ben Halston…"

"Is my dad," he said, and when she frowned, he revised for accuracy. "Adoptive dad, actually. Drew and Zac are my brothers. You've met them?"

"Uh-huh." She studied him for a moment. "Sam Calhoun. You're the reporter. The one who gave a false—"

"Yeah, yeah. Now come on," Sam said impatiently when the glow of her flashlight revealed a flare of sympathy in her sea-green eyes. He did *not* want sympathy. "The kids?" he added, hoping that would get her moving.

"Right." Tiny strawberry blond curls, at least the short strands not covered by her ridiculous hat, bobbed around her face as she nodded. "I've turned off the water and the power so there's no danger of fire."

"The house doesn't matter. It can be fixed. Kids can't." He frowned at her. "Well?"

"Coming." She took a step, stumbled on something buried under the snow and grabbed her leg with a grimace. "Ow. That stupid sled. I told them to put it away."

Exhaling his frustration when the storm brushed snow across his face a second time, Sam scooped all five-foot-nothing of her into his arms and carried her and the suitcase she clutched toward her children.

"Wait a minute, I—"

"Come on, guys. Into the car," Sam ordered, ignoring Joy's protests.

"What's wrong with Mom?" the littlest one, Cris, asked with a worried expression.

"She hurt her foot. Just get in, okay?" He nodded his thanks when Josh opened the front passenger door and set Joy on the seat. He waited until she put her suitcase on the floor at her feet before he closed the door. After ensuring the children were safely belted in, Sam shook the snow off his bare head and climbed into the driver's seat, grateful for the warmth pouring from the dash and wishing he'd bought a down-filled jacket when he'd passed through JFK on his way home to his family at Hanging Hearts Ranch. "Okay, Joy Grainger. Where to?"

"You tell me," she said, her voice sharp.

"Sorry?" Sam blinked in confusion. Where had the anger come from? He stared at her, noticing without meaning to that, minus the outrageous hat which now rested in her lap, the curls curved around her heart-shaped face like a caress. Many women preferred long hair, but the short style that hugged Joy's cheeks and framed her green eyes certainly suited her gamine features.

"I left a message for your father, my *landlord*," she emphasized. "That was a week ago. I told him that tree was in danger of falling. I left him another message about it yesterday. He never returned my calls." She glared at him, sparks flashing from her glacial irises, revealing her obvious fury.

"Um, Dad—"

"Now the tree has fallen, just as I said it would," she continued, completely ignoring his attempt to explain, "leaving us without a place to stay, in the midst of a blizzard. Nor do I have a vehicle to drive. And I need both a house and a car in order to live."

Sam was used to making split-second decisions. Sometimes his life had depended on it, but the last one he'd made had cost him his career. Since then he'd vowed never to decide anything in a hurry ever again. Still, one look out the window told him this storm wasn't weakening. They sure couldn't sit here for the night. So he made his decision and whipped his car into gear.

"Where are we going?" the lady demanded, her tone as chilly as that vicious north wind out there. "Are you putting us up at Sunshine's hotel?"

"Nope." Sam edged back onto the highway and flicked his lights to bright. He sure hoped he didn't meet any traffic because the lanes were getting blown in.

"You should take us there," Joy insisted, her tone sharply accusing. "We're your father's tenants and this happened because of his negligence—where *are* we going?"

"Hanging Hearts Ranch." Sam figured patience wasn't Joy's strong suit, judging by the way she fidgeted. But then, she had three kids to worry about. "Relax. It's not very far from here."

"The Double H? I know where it is." She drew back against her seat as if he'd grown horns. "We can't go there!"

"We can and we are." Sam steered around a big drift and plowed on. "There's a log cabin that's warm and safe where you and your kids can bed down and get some rest for as long as it takes me to figure out what to do about the house."

"You?" Her sea-foam eyes darkened to emerald. "What has our situation got to do with you?"

"It's me, not Dad, who's your actual landlord," Sam admitted with an inner wince. There went his privacy.

"Pardon?" Joy frowned. "You mean you own our house?"

"Afraid so. Dad manages the property for me when I can't be here. I was working overseas until—"

"Until you got fired for giving that report that was a lie."

She sure didn't mince words. Well, nobody else had either. In fact, he'd been inundated with savage com-

ments and vicious personal attacks ever since he'd been
released from captivity.

"Yes. Until I got fired for lying, Joy." Sam turned
through the gate, flinching as the ranch's arched metal
sign hanging above them screeched in the wind. "I apologize that Dad didn't respond to your calls. It's not that he
didn't care. He's been in the hospital with pneumonia."

"I'm so sorry," she whispered. Her cheeks had turned
an embarrassed shade of red, though maybe that was
from the cold. "I hadn't heard."

"Doesn't matter," he said brusquely. "I'll make sure
your house gets fixed. Insurance should cover your car,
but if it doesn't, I'll fix that, too." Compared to the other
things Sam had to fix, like making sure his source was
still alive, Joy's problems seemed minimal. "For now,
let's get everyone inside the cabin."

Sam urged Joy and her kids up the stairs and into
the cheery log home that had been built years earlier. In
the stone fireplace, logs crackled merrily, adding heat,
and chasing away the chilly gust that had pushed inside
with them.

His brothers were expecting him, and it looked like
they'd made the cabin warm and welcoming. Sam figured
this little family would have everything they needed here.

"Oh." He paused. "I never thought— Your husband?
Should I go get him?" He hated the idea of a second trip
out in this savage storm, but he'd do it if necessary. *Because now you're really involved*, his brain scoffed.

"We don't got a daddy," Cris said soberly. "He died."

Sam's brain replayed memories of his own birth parents' deaths when he was about Becca's age. He and his
brothers had been taken in by the Halstons here, on this
same ranch, many years ago. Hanging Hearts had become their home.

"Someone was expecting *you* to stay here, Sam." Joy glanced around. "There's a Christmas tree and decorations. You were coming home for Christmas, to this," she guessed, her eyes searching his. She shook her head firmly. "We can't take your place."

"It's not a problem. There's lots of room at the main house. I'll stay there until I get things sorted out." Sam held out his hand for her jacket, thinking as he hung it up that it felt more suited for autumn than a winter blizzard. When the kids had shrugged out of their coats and kicked off their boots, he smiled at them. "Did you guys have supper before the tree fell?"

Three heads moved left and then right.

"They're fine. I brought some snacks." Joy grabbed the suitcase he'd carried in and opened it. She gave a packet of peanuts to each kid, though Sam noted there wasn't one for her.

Her gesture lit a flicker of admiration inside him— unselfish, just like his mom. Mothers everywhere always put their family's welfare before their own. He'd done a story on that…

"Why don't you save those nuts for dessert?" he suggested, tamping down the past. "My nose is telling me someone left something yummy in the oven." He peeked in through the glass door. "Chicken potpie, if I'm not mistaken," he said as he glanced over one shoulder.

Three children licked their lips, glanced guiltily at their mom, and quickly resumed their blank expressions. She'd trained them not to look needy. Sam understood that. Covering the poorest parts of the world had taught him that no mom ever wanted to admit the shame of being unable to feed her child, even though it usually wasn't her fault.

"Want to set the table, guys?" Sam grinned as the kids

rushed to obey. "Let's see what's in the fridge. A salad. Good. You can add your peanuts to that if you want." He scanned the cabinets. "Fresh loaf of bread here, with butter. Oh, yum. Peach pie for dessert. Everything's ready. Mind if I sit down and eat with you? I'm starved."

"I'm sure no one expected you'd have four extra mouths to feed." Joy shot her kids a look, which Sam translated as a warning not to eat too much.

"Maybe they didn't *expect* you," he agreed calmly as he poured three large glasses of milk. "But in my case, they'd consider leftovers a necessity because chicken potpie is my favorite. Don't worry, Joy, there's plenty for all of us and then some."

Sam flicked the switch on the already prepared coffee maker and inhaled the brewing fragrance while waiting for Joy to tell her children where to sit. He'd missed this little log house. And American coffee. He'd missed feeling like he belonged, and the security of being on familiar land, where nobody could make him do or say anything he didn't want to. Most of all, Sam had missed being accepted.

The role of outcast was a lonely one.

Noting Josh lick his lips, Sam shook off his gloomy thoughts and carefully lifted the potpie out of the oven. He set it proudly on a hot mat on the table, as if it was his own creation.

"Think that will do us?" He chuckled at the four sets of very wide eyes, all of them that same sea-foam-green shade. "Who wants some?"

Surprisingly, the children remained silent.

"Is it okay if we say grace first?" Joy asked quietly.

"Of course. That's a necessity in our family, too." Sam sat and bowed his head, ashamed that he'd needed the reminder. But when you were used to grabbing something while in pursuit of a story or running for your life, saying grace often got left out. Probably one of the reasons God now felt so distant.

"Thank You, Father, for this meal and this lovely home. We ask that You bless us and be with those in the storm. Amen." Joy lifted her strawberry-blond head and met his gaze with a smile. "We very much appreciate you coming home for Christmas, Sam. We especially appreciate that you chose tonight to return."

"Glad to be of service," he said, quoting his dad's favorite homily. "Let's eat."

It took some doing, but he finally got the kids chatting freely between mouthfuls.

"So, Josh, you're eight going on nine. Becca's five, and Cris?" Sam waited while the little boy chewed his last crust of bread. "Let me guess? Four?"

Cris nodded his flaxen head. "Uh-huh."

They ate in silence for a few minutes without questioning him. Sam didn't mind. He didn't want to explain about his past. Not now. Not ever.

"Who wants some peach pie?" he said.

The kids did not respond.

"You don't want pie? Are you guys for real?" Figuring they were embarrassed or thought there wouldn't be enough, Sam got some plates and cut a slice. "I don't know who made it, but this looks and smells delicious."

"It's Mom's," Josh told him.

"Huh?" Sam frowned at Joy. "You brought a pie in that suitcase?"

The kids giggled.

"Josh means it came from my bakery. That's my mark in the middle of the crust." Joy smiled. "The children have already eaten peach pie three times this week, so they're probably tired of it."

"Who gets tired of peach pie?" Sam asked in disbelief. "Not me." He took a bite, closed his eyes, and let the tangy flavor roll over his tongue. "Delicious. Cinnamon and a tiny hint of nutmeg. "What bakery?"

"Yes, cinnamon and a few other spices," Joy agreed before grimacing. "My bakery. I run—*ran* a bakery from our home. The bakery in Sunshine closed last year. That's why we moved here. I've been trying to negotiate with a company called Possibilities, who bought the old bakery building."

She took a sip of her coffee while the big lump in Sam's throat expanded until he was almost choking.

"I want to rent the building and equipment from them so I can reopen it," Joy told him calmly.

"I see," he finally managed to croak. "And?"

"And nothing. Everything is on hold because Possibilities hasn't responded to any of my letters. If they don't answer me pretty soon, I'll have to look elsewhere." Disappointment dimmed her eyes.

"I see." *Oh, boy, you're in trouble,* Sam's brain chided. *You should have come home sooner.*

"Waiting so long for a response is why I had my kitchen at our house—*your* house—" she corrected "—certified by the health department. Until I can find something else to rent, I've been baking there to fill the orders I get."

"Ah." Now he understood her earlier irritation.

"At least, I *was* doing that. Until that tree fell." Worry wrinkled her brow. "I don't know what happens now. I only know that bakery building would have been perfect. With the Christmas season coming, I could have…" Her shoulders drooped. "It doesn't matter now."

"Mom can't bake in our house anymore," Josh muttered.

"'Cause it's bwoken," Becca explained.

"It sure is." Sam grimaced.

There'd been too many emails, too many scathing comments and demeaning castigations filling his inbox. Sam had stopped reading them because he just couldn't take it anymore. Now he wished he hadn't. Obviously he'd missed some information from his dad explaining about his rental house. If he'd read his emails, he might have been able to save Joy and her kids all this hassle.

"It's my fault you're in this situation. I apologize."

"No, it isn't. It's the tree's fault," she said, barely managing a smile.

"Whatever." He wouldn't let himself off the hook so easily. "I'm really sorry, Joy. I'd planned to be back home before Thanksgiving. I thought I'd have time to check on your place and make sure it was ready for winter, but I failed." *Again.* He paused, frowned. "Can you bake tomorrow's orders here?"

"I don't have any supplies," she said as she glanced around. "But assuming I got some from my place and the oven works, I guess I could manage."

"But?" He knew there was one because of her frown.

"You see, the thing is, I have a big party order to fill for the weekend. I doubt..." She left her thought hanging as she surveyed the small kitchen, obviously running scenarios in her head.

Sam guessed Joy didn't want to discuss it with her children present, listening to every word, so he rose and began clearing their dishes. The kids quickly pitched in, obviously having done it before. Josh was a master at loading the dishwasher, and soon the house was back in order.

"If only I could have gotten into the old Bits and Bites bakery building," Joy said, her tone slightly sour, nodding when he held up the coffeepot. He refilled their cups as she continued, "If I could have persuaded Possibilities to let me rent immediately, I'd have plenty of space. Besides that, all the equipment I need to make my bakery dream come true is already there, waiting to be used."

"Ah." What could Sam say to that? He wished he'd read his email.

"The lawyer for Possibilities has ignored my letters. They refuse to even give me a chance." Her eyes glistened like icicles in sunlight.

"Bits and Bites—that was the name of the bakery? The big building beside an empty lot on the corner, across from the bank?" Sam clarified. Joy nodded. "It wasn't called that last time I was home," he mused.

"I think the previous owners only ran it for a short time before they had trouble and let it go back to the bank. Apparently it was then bought by Possibilities. I can't figure out how to talk to whomever Possibilities is." Her lips pursed.

"If you could, what would you say to them?" Sam asked, and then wondered if he should have.

"I'd give them an earful about *possibilities*," Joy shot back. "This town *needs* a bakery. The more businesses Sunshine loses, the sooner folks will leave and— Sorry," she apologized suddenly, looking embarrassed. "I didn't mean to dump on you."

"No problem. And as it happens, I agree with you. Sunshine must remain vital, with plenty of businesses, for it to survive. That's something I've been—" He stopped, grimaced. "Now I'm dumping."

Joy's words clearly echoed Sam's own private vision for his hometown. That was the very reason he had begun buying old buildings and renovating them, to try to coax new business into town. He'd always had this desire for Sunshine to remain attractive, a good place to do business, so that it wouldn't fail like so many other small towns nearby had. He'd given a lot of thought to how the town could do that. But he didn't need to blurt it all out now.

"What are you so quiet about?" Joy murmured.

"Trying to remember." He studied her, once more admiring the sheen on her hair in the flickering firelight. "I thought I heard something about a wonky floor in that bakery building."

"It's an original wooden floor, from the early fifties. Of course it's wonky! That's part of the charm." Joy sounded irritated. Her nails tapping against the table added to that impression. "Nobody erects a big expansive building like that anymore or puts in those massive storefront windows. They would be perfect for display or a little coffee nook. I haven't been able to get inside recently, but I'm sure there's enough room in the basement for a Mother's Day cake-decorating event for kids, or catering, or…"

"Wow! You have plans," Sam said, his respect for her growing.

"Fat lot of good they do me now. My bakery dreams collapsed when that tree fell." She shook it off before rising. "Okay, kids. It looks like we're staying here tonight, so it's time to get ready for bed. Pj's are in the suitcase, along with toothbrushes. Take turns nicely."

As if he'd been assigned the task, Josh shepherded his siblings toward the bathroom. Joy faced Sam, her luminous face enhanced by the glow from the Christmas tree. Beautiful, but so weary.

"I'm sorry not to sound more grateful for your help," she apologized, summoning a smile. "It's just that lately I can't seem to catch a break. I'd really hoped to get my bakery going before Christmas. I'll just have to keep praying about it, I guess."

"Do that. I will, too." Sam remembered as he said it

that he hadn't been able to pray for a while. Ever since he'd been captured... He shoved that thought away as a new idea began to percolate. "Rest tonight."

"That's easy to say," Joy mumbled.

"Try to let it all go for the next few hours," he advised gently. "In the morning we'll go back to your place and see what we can salvage so you can get back to baking. All is not lost yet, Mrs. Baker."

"I wish I dared to believe that." She turned away so he wouldn't see her secret delight at his nickname for her.

"Is there anyone you need to contact?" Sam asked softly. "Family?"

Family? Sadness welled inside but Joy tamped it down.

"No family. It's just me and my kids." This man didn't need to know her sad history.

"I was an orphan, too," Sam told her, his voice thoughtful. "Our parents were killed in a car accident near here. After some surgeries, Ben and Bonnie nursed us back to health then brought us here to Hanging Hearts Ranch and adopted the three of us Calhoun boys."

"I've met them. They're very kind." She gulped then blurted, "I'm not an orphan, though. My parents disowned me."

"Oh. Why?" His calm, quiet question helped Joy regain control.

She figured his ability to empathize was probably the reason why Sam had been so effective at reporting. Except for that last time...

"Joy? You don't have to tell me if you don't want."

"No, it's okay. It's old history. I got pregnant right after high school," she said, still embarrassed to admit her mistake. "I thought I could make it right by marrying Nick, though my parents insisted he wasn't trustworthy. But I was stubborn. They said they'd disown me if I married him. I did, and they've kept their word. I haven't seen or heard from them in a long time. They won't even respond to my letters." She scowled. "It's galling to admit, but it turns out they were right about Nick, too."

"That doesn't make it any easier," Sam commiserated with a frown. "Surely if they knew about your kids, they'd want to get to know their grandchildren?"

"I thought that, too, so I went to see them once." She remembered that dark day so well. "It was right after Nick was killed. He'd left us to live his dream, at the circus," she explained. "He was killed three days later by an angry elephant. I was pregnant with Cris. I thought maybe if my parents knew I'd been widowed they'd forgive me, but they told me to go away."

"I'm so sorry, Joy." Sam's hand covered hers.

"Yeah. Me, too." She huffed out a sigh of regret and then shrugged it off. "Their loss. My kids are amazing."

"Yes, they are," he agreed with a grin. She liked him very much for saying that, but she still withdrew her hand from his.

Becca appeared, holding her precious though ragged teddy bear.

"Teeth clean, face and hands washed, sweetie?" she asked her only daughter.

"Uh-huh." Becca hugged her leg. "I'm gonna pway, too, Mommy. 'Cause God loves us, wight?"

"Yes, He does, darling." Joy hugged her little girl, striving to regain her brave face. "You and Cris find my Bible in the suitcase and we'll read a story before bed, just as soon as Josh is ready. You guys decide which one."

When Becca dashed away calling the others to come, Joy chuckled.

"What's so funny?" Sam asked, eyes wide.

"She'll ask the others to choose Daniel in the lions' den. For Cris. He loves that story." Her smile faltered. "I think it's tied up with him not having a dad. Cris tries so hard to be brave."

"Don't we all?" Sam's face suddenly altered, making her think he was reminded of something horrible in his past. Then he jumped up, grabbed his coat off the hook and thrust his arms into it. "I'll let you get on with bedtime then."

"Thank you for everything, Sam. We really appreciate it." Joy gnawed on her bottom lip. "I don't know what we would have done—"

"You would have managed because that's what you moms always do. I'm in awe of your managerial abilities." He grinned and she knew he was trying to lighten the atmosphere. "Please don't worry about anything. There's a way to fix this and I will find it. If you need anything in the night, there's an intercom system in the master bedroom. Press the red button and I'll answer. Okay?" He waited for her assent.

"Thank you, Sam." Joy nodded. "I promise, we won't be staying here long. I'll figure this out and stand on my own two feet again. Soon." Her smile felt forced. "Till then I'm truly grateful for everything you've done."

"My pleasure. Good night." Sam left his car outside her door and walked across the snowy yard to the main house, where he disappeared inside.

Joy peered out the window. Through the gusts of whirling snowflakes, she eventually caught the flickering light of a fire illuminating a room in the big house. She figured Sam must be tired if he'd been traveling for a while. She'd heard about his recent return from the Middle East. That's where he'd made that false report, wasn't it? She couldn't help wondering if other reporters' diatribes she'd heard against Sam actually told the whole story about his recent firing from his longtime network. Or was there more to it and the business in the Middle East than had been publicized?

"Mommy?"

"Coming." Joy read the kids their story, prayed with each one and then tucked them into bed, so grateful they were snug and warm and safe tonight.

But what about tomorrow?

"I'm trying to learn to trust You, but I just can't see a way out of this, God," she prayed when she was once more alone and seated in front of the fire. "Please show me."

After a while her thoughts drifted back to Sam. The well-known journalist who had frequently appeared on television with heart-wrenching human-interest stories had been a favorite of hers for years. Sam Calhoun covered a story honestly. He didn't embellish or pretend or make up news. He gave the facts, but in a way that reached out and grabbed your heart.

Until that last story. The way he'd presented it had been so unlike him: cold, almost detached, as if he was reading someone else's work. What could have happened to make him file a story so easily proven false? And why hadn't he immediately corrected his report, made an excuse, or explained to his many viewers why he'd done it?

In the six weeks that followed his erroneous coverage, Sam Calhoun hadn't clarified anything. Not that it mattered, because by the time he appeared in public, he'd already been vilified by the very colleagues and agencies who'd sung his praises and awarded him for his work mere weeks earlier. His disgrace seemed total when even his own network had publicly disowned him.

Now Sam was home. He must feel embarrassed and ashamed about his illustrious career derailing so publicly. Maybe he'd returned to lick his wounds or maybe he was home for good. Only—what would a world-class journalist do on Hanging Hearts Ranch?

Stop thinking about Sam Calhoun! He'll probably leave soon anyway. Focus on your future, her brain chastised.

Joy pulled a pad of paper close and began making a list. But half an hour later her mind still hadn't let go of the lean, tanned, six-foot reporter with the melting coffee eyes and shaggy brown hair who'd rescued her and her kids in the storm. Funny how she'd known immediately that she could trust Sam Calhoun.

And that was a problem. Joy couldn't afford to trust another man. She was a single parent to three children and entirely on her own. That wasn't going to change. It had taken her almost five years to recover financially from Nick's abandonment of her. Healing mentally from the knowledge that a man she'd loved had dumped her and his kids—whom he'd professed to love with his whole heart— would take Joy a lot longer to forget. The only good thing about it all was that she had learned a hard lesson.

Depend on no one but God. The only way to make it through life was to be strong, to make your dreams come true yourself. Even a stranger's helping hand in a dire emergency would not dissuade her from that path.

Chapter Two

Joy rose at 5:30 a.m. For the past hour she'd worked quickly but as silently as possible. Now she needed a break. With her warm coffee mug snuggled against her cheek, she swiveled her gaze from the clock to the pans of cooling shortbread, and then to the scribbles across her notepad on the table.

Her heart sank to her toes. She'd gone over and over the figures. Earlier this morning, using supplies she'd found here, she'd baked enough shortbread to fill three orders. But that wouldn't be nearly enough to meet her obligations.

Thanks to a stupid tree, the unresponsiveness of a company called Possibilities and the neglect of her home's owner—that was Sam, she remembered glumly—her venture as Sunshine's newest baker was over.

"Now what, Lord?" she whispered and then waited for some heavenly guidance.

A very gentle tap on the door roused her. She walked over and opened it. Sam Calhoun and a young woman stood on the step.

"Good morning. Joy, this is Kira. She's a junior wrangler here on the ranch, but she also helps out with my brothers' kids in a pinch."

"Come in." Joy stood back to let them inside her borrowed home, not sure exactly why she needed to know this girl, but very thankful she'd taken the time after she'd risen to comb her hair and dab on some makeup, before Sam's arrival.

She refused to consider why that mattered.

"Kira's going to stay with the kids while you and I drive over to the house and retrieve whatever you need to start, or, should I say, to *keep* baking," he said with a glance at the cookies. "We should be there and back before the kids wake up. But if there's a problem, Kira has my phone number and she'll call."

"Right away," the young woman promised with a big smile. "If you're not back, I'll make breakfast for them and be sure they're ready for school. I do that for Sam's brothers' kids all the time when they need me." When she smiled, her freckles stood out against her white teeth.

"I'm not sure—"

"I'm not sure either, Joy. But the only way to be sure is to go take a look. Agreed?" Sam lifted her coat off the hook and held it out for her to slip her arms inside. "Gloves?"

"In my pocket." She tugged on her boots, half-bemused and not really certain what this trip was going to accomplish. But if there was even the sliver of a chance she could keep her business operating, she had to grab it.

"Good to go?" Sam tilted his head to one side when she nodded. "I was kind of hoping you'd wear the hat again."

She rolled her eyes.

"That's a no?" He shrugged. "Shoot. That hat would have come in handy. Well, we'll just hope and pray a bear hasn't stopped by to taste your supplies."

"A bear?" Joy gulped. She'd never even given wild

animals a thought in the three months she'd lived in the semi-isolated house.

"Kidding. Let's go." He ushered her outside then turned to Kira. "Phone if you need to."

"We'll be fine," Kira promised.

Joy started down the stairs then stopped, surprised to see two other men waiting near a red crew cab truck with Hanging Hearts Ranch painted in white on its side.

"I think you've met my brothers, Drew and Zac," Sam explained. "They'll give us a hand moving whatever you need. One thing about being a Calhoun—you can always call on your brothers for help, no matter how early it is."

"Best not push that too far, Sam." One of the men waggled a warning finger. "There's always payback."

Both men said good morning to Joy, tipped their Stetsons and politely waited by an open truck door for her to climb into the front seat. Next to Sam, she noted with a gulp.

They were a handsome trio, these Calhoun men; all three tall, lean, and dashing. But Sam won first place in the looks department for his cute, mussed-up appearance and those bittersweet chocolate eyes—what woman didn't love chocolate?—framed by incredibly long, thick lashes. That whole picture was enhanced by his mouth, perpetually, it seemed, curved into a smile that did funny things to her heart rate.

Not that Joy was interested in Sam. Oh, no. She didn't have either the time or the desire for romance. Men were trouble and she did not need more trouble. She had enough to do just trying to keep her business going and care for her family.

"Your cookies smelled awesome. You must have been up very early. Tired?" Sam asked, drawing her out of her thoughts.

"No. Just—wondering what we'll find," she said. "I hope there's not too much structural damage. For your sake," she added, lest he think she was being selfish.

"The house is insured. Don't worry about that," he reassured her. "I think it's more important to get your baking business operating again."

"But—" She hesitated before blurting, "I can't keep staying in your cabin. We have to find someplace to live."

"Why can't you stay there?" Zac leaned forward. "Is there something wrong with the place?"

"No, it's wonderful," she said quickly. "But it's where Sam planned to stay. We're taking his space."

The two men in the back scoffed at that.

"Trust us, Sam's better off in the main house, where Mom's got the freezer so jammed full of food, all he has to do is put it in the microwave," Drew said.

"Sam's a horrible cook," Zac added.

"Not true," Sam protested, though he didn't seem upset by their comments.

"Let me rephrase." Zac faked a cough. "Sam can cook, but the mess he makes is a nightmare. We used to hate it when it was his turn to make dinner because cleanup lasted till bedtime."

"Focusing on the house now," Sam reminded everyone as he pulled up in front of it. "Whoa!"

"Vast understatement, especially for a guy who uses words to earn his living," Drew joked, but he, too, sounded stunned by what he saw.

With the sun's rays not quite cresting, the house looked like a scary movie scene with its jagged roofline and branches sticking out all over. It appeared far worse now than it had looked in the storm of last night. The men's sudden silence told Joy this was not going to be the easy fix she'd prayed for.

"Let's take a look," Zac suggested quietly as he opened his truck door.

"Would you mind staying put for a few minutes, Joy? Just until we make sure it's safe inside?" Sam's darkening brown eyes echoed the grim downward twist of his lips.

"Okay." She gulped. She hadn't even thought of the place falling around her ears when she'd been in there last night.

"Won't be long." Sam exited the vehicle, but left it running with the heat on.

Joy watched as the brothers tromped through the snow, pointing and calling out to each other as they walked around to the left. It felt like an hour passed as she waited nervously for their return.

About ready to jump out and inspect the place herself, Joy sighed in relief when two of the Calhoun brothers finally reappeared on the opposite side of the house. Sam shook his head at Drew, who pointed and talked. After a few moments they seemed to come to some agreement and Sam returned to the truck.

"Well?" she asked when he was inside, warming his hands against the vent.

"You can't go in," he said firmly.

"But I have to—"

Sam whipped the truck into gear.

"Wait! What about your broth—" She stopped when she realized he was turning around so the truck's rear faced the house.

Then there was a thud as Drew pulled down the tailgate. Zac appeared and pushed in a heaping box of stuff.

"We're going to take out what we can today, like the food and whatever else you want. Anything you don't need will go into a storage container that Drew will order.

Okay?" As Sam waited for her response, she noted the strain on his face.

"It's that bad?" Joy whispered. Horrified when he nodded, she whispered, "Tell me."

"A beam fell last night. I guess the weight of the tree was too much, or maybe the initial fall damaged some rafters." Sam gulped and then continued in a very subdued tone. "The beam fell across two of the bedrooms. If you and the kids had been in there…" He shook his head. "Thank God you got them out."

"And that you came along," she added with a shudder. "If—"

"Let's not think about what-ifs now," he suggested. "The important thing is to get what you need and move on." He opened his door.

"Sam?" When he turned to face her, Joy asked, "Can I carry some things? You could hand them to me so I wouldn't need to go in."

He shrugged. "If you want, but you don't have to."

"I'll feel better doing something." Joy got out of the truck and walked around the side of the house. "Tell them not to bother with anything liquid," she said when she spied Zac through the window, examining her flavoring supplies. "Most lose their usefulness when frozen, and it was pretty cold last night. They're garbage."

"How about you tell me what you want and I'll bring it out?" Sam suggested.

"Good idea." She began listing items. "None of the canned stuff. It could be spoiled. I'll take all the flour. It's in a big silver tin. There should be sugar in a matching tin beside it and a couple more bags of it on the supply shelf in the pantry. I also need the mixing bowls and my big mixer."

Sam left to retrieve them while Joy mentally sorted

through her stock. After he came back and had pushed his load into the truck bed, she was ready.

"I'll take everything in the fridge and the freezer. Also, the baking pans and the rack they're on, if it's still any good. All the pots and pans." She mentally cast her eyes around the space. "The big drawer on the end has my spoons and utensils, which I'll need. Oh, and my packaging containers. I'll want them to fill orders. They're in the porch. They have *Joy's Treats* printed on the side."

They sorted and loaded things as the sun slowly rose. When Sam emerged with an armload of clothes, Joy offered a suggestion.

"Why not just dump all the kids' clothes in their suitcases? There are large navy ones under each of their beds."

"You want to come in and get your own things, though, don't you?" Sam sighed when she nodded. "Can't blame you. Okay. We've stabilized the place somewhat but walk carefully. A lot of snow has blown in and the floors are slippery." After ensuring her room was safe, he left her there, but not before warning, "Five minutes. That's all you're getting."

"Sam?" She hated to ask but it was important to her.

"Yeah?" He faced her, Stetson pushed back on his head, looking lean, competent and in control. That made it easier to ask.

"There's a box under the sofa in the living room. It's full of pictures and memorabilia of my kids." She stopped, hesitated. "Would you be able to— That is, do you think…"

"I'll find it," he promised and then tapped his watch. "Four minutes left."

She'd just stuffed the last bit of her clothing into a garbage bag when he pushed his head around the door.

"Time's up."

"I'm finished." Joy released the bag into his outstretched hand and accepted his other hand to help navigate the area around her bed where the tree had deposited a big branch.

But outside, when she saw the truck bed piled helter-skelter with her things, a lump lodged in her throat. All her work to make this place their home, and now it was… No! She couldn't think like that. This would be their fresh start.

"Strikes me that we didn't pack any toys," Drew murmured, rubbing his chin. "If you'll tell me where they are, I can retrieve a few. Kids need toys."

"Listen to Mr. Father here," Zac teased. "You've been a daddy, what, two years? And now you're the fount of knowledge?"

"Yep." Drew grinned as he crossed his arms over his chest. "I'm a fast learner."

"Joy?" Sam frowned as he studied her. "Toys? Are they in the shed?"

She was embarrassed by how few unbroken toys her children owned. She simply hadn't had the money to spend on them. Nor did she have enough now to buy them new ones for Christmas presents this year. But she'd put on a brave face and pretend or these men would feel sorry for her and Joy did not want their pity. Especially not Sam's.

"I took some toys with us last night," she said. "There are only a couple of snow-sliding mats in the shed. They're wrecked, but the kids did have some wooden toys in a metal box on the floor by the sofa. They could use those." The words had barely left her mouth when Zac and Drew disappeared around the side of the house. "This is so nice of you all," she began then gasped. "Oh!"

"What?" Sam studied her. "I know you want to see your kids off to school this morning, so you better talk fast. What did you just remember?"

"There's a navy bag tucked on the very top shelf of my closet, at the back. I need to get it." She started walking toward the house but Sam grabbed her arm.

"I'll find it. You get in the truck and warm up."

"No! I have to get it myself." She tried to ease free, but just then a branch cracked and fell, smashing a window.

Sam seemed to freeze. His face blanched and his fists clenched at his sides. He stared at the house, his expression revealing his alarm.

Concerned, Joy stepped forward and touched his shoulder. "Sam?"

He reared away at her touch, glazed eyes staring at her. Several moments passed before he seemed to shake off his dazed state and refocus.

"Get in the truck," he ordered before he took off running toward the house yelling, "Zac! Drew! Everything okay?"

Confused by what had just happened, Joy watched him disappear, wondering what had caused him to zone out like that. But she was also scared. Because of her, these wonderful men might be hurt. She sent a plea heavenward while her gaze remained glued to the house.

Finally the three brothers reappeared, laughing about something. Sam looked as if the earlier incident where he'd spaced out had never happened as he handed her the bag that contained the money she hadn't had time to deposit.

While they drove away, she tucked the precious bag in her pocket. "What was so funny?" she asked.

"Drew scared a skunk," Sam told her, chuckling.

"When that branch fell, the skunk was more afraid than we were and left. Fast."

"Otherwise I'd be walking back to the Double H," Drew assured her dryly.

"Because skunk aroma is killer," Zac clarified when she frowned in confusion.

"Oh." Joy felt dumb.

The three men didn't pay her much attention as they teased each other on the short ride back to the house. They quickly carried in her supplies while Joy explained to her startled children that from now on they'd be riding the bus to school from the ranch.

"After school you'll get off here, not our old place," she reminded Josh when Kira had left. She kissed him and Becca, told them to have a good day and watched as they raced out to the waiting school bus looking care-free, as if this was a new adventure she'd arranged spe-cifically for their enjoyment. "Now you and I must get to work," she told Cris.

"Zac and Drew have taken your big stuff to an empty storage shed we have here," Sam explained. "There's too much for you to store in here, but we can retrieve it whenever you want."

"Thank you." She hadn't noticed the other men leave, hadn't even said thank-you. These Calhouns were amaz-ing.

"You didn't have breakfast, right, Joy? How about we have some toast before you start baking?" Sam suggested. "I'm guessing you'll need more baking supplies, too." He plopped four slices of bread into the toaster.

"I guess," she agreed and checked the fridge. "I used some of your eggs, flour and butter for the shortbread. There's still some left of each. I have what you brought from my place, too, so I could get started on a couple of cake orders, I suppose." She liked the way Sam didn't wait to be served. He saw a need and got to work filling it.

"I have to go into town. If you give me a list, I'll pick up whatever groceries you need while I'm there," he said, slathering butter on the now brown toast. "Want peanut butter, too?"

"Yes, please. And thank you." His absence would give her time to get refocused on baking and decide what orders she could fill and which she'd have to cancel. "It will take me a minute to make a list."

"No rush." Sam put the toast on the table and sat down next to Cris. While they ate, she scribbled a list of what she needed and he chatted with her son. Joy was almost finished when Sam rose to pour her another cup of coffee.

"Can Cris come with me?" He met her surprised glance with a grin. "Don't worry. I'll borrow a car seat for him. From Abby. She's Zac's wife."

"Do you want to go?" Joy asked Cris, chastising herself for thinking that she could get so much more done if she didn't have to entertain her young son. When Cris eagerly nodded, she sought Sam's gaze and found it on her. "I guess he could. If he won't be too much trouble."

"He won't be," Sam insisted with a wink at the boy. "We'll have fun. List ready? Then come on, Cris. Let's get your jacket."

He finished his coffee, then gathered the dishes and loaded the dishwasher while Joy helped her son dress for the winter weather. She tried to give Sam money for the groceries, but he insisted it would be easier if he bought them and gave her the bill later. She stood by the window, watching as the big man helped her young son down the stairs and into the waiting vehicle, which someone had driven over after installing a booster seat.

It had been a long time since Joy had allowed her kids

to go anywhere with anyone other than her. Funny how it felt okay to let Cris go with Sam. She mulled over that for a few minutes, trying to understand why, until she realized she was wasting precious time thinking about Sam again when she should be working.

But as Joy mixed cakes and cooked squares to fill today's special orders, she couldn't get her mind off the good-looking, easygoing reporter who seemed so conscientious about her and the kids. He'd gone totally above and beyond for them.

So why did Joy feel she wasn't seeing the real Sam, that he was hiding something?

Why would he do that?

"I'm sorry to bug you, Jerry. I know you city guys don't like to come out here in winter, but I need the house assessed right away. I have a hunch you'll tell me it's a write-off, but at least once the insurance forms are under way, I can think about the next move." Sam listened to the other man's agreement before ending the call. "You okay?" he asked Cris, surprised the little boy had left most of his doughnut uneaten.

"Uh-huh." The boy pushed away his plate. "My mom's are better."

"Mine was dry, too." Sam finished his coffee and tossed some bills on the table. "I've got one more errand. Ready to go?"

Cris squeezed out of the booth and zipped up his coat in response. Out on the street, Sam wasn't sure if it was apropos to hold a four-year-old's hand. But when Cris's mittened fingers slid into his, he felt a flush of pleasure.

"I have to talk to a man and it might take a little while." He directed Cris into the general store. "But this place has a great area with lots of toys for kids to play with. Promise not to wander away?"

"Okay." Cris's eyes grew into round orbs when he saw the children's play area. He unzipped his coat, tossed it onto a pint-sized chair and immediately headed for the big yellow dump truck sitting on a shelf.

"I'll be nearby if you need me, Cris. And I'll check on you, so don't think I've left you here." Joy probably wouldn't have left her child here to play, but Sam needed to talk to the owner privately. "Okay?"

"Uh-huh." Cris gazed in awe at the truck.

Still Sam hesitated to leave the boy by himself, until a smiling woman he recognized hailed him.

"Hello, Sam. I'm so glad you're safely home."

"Thanks, Miss Partridge. How are you?" The town's now retired librarian beamed as she shook his hand. *Please don't let her ask me a bunch of questions, God. You know I can't talk about it, not until everyone's safe. Anyway, I need to figure out what You want me to do now.*

"Why, I'm fine as frog's hair, dear." She glanced at Cris. "I heard what you said, Sam. You go ahead and do your business. I'll keep an eye on this young fellow for you," she promised. "He's Joy Grainger's son, isn't he? How do you two know each other?"

"We met last night." He was surprised by the question. Miss Partridge usually knew everything that happened in Sunshine before anyone else did. He chided himself for feeling a smug sense of satisfaction that for once, he knew more than she did. "I was driving past when I noticed her kids standing in the yard. The storm damaged her house."

"Oh, no. How awful. Is she all right?" Miss Partridge asked.

"Everyone's fine. I took her and her kids to the ranch

to stay at the log house until she can work something out," Sam explained. "I want to talk to Marty, see if he can hazard a guess as to how long repairs will take. Joy needs to know."

Sam and his father had long ago agreed to keep Sam's ownership of the local properties he bought through his company private, so it was unlikely Miss Partridge knew he owned Joy's house, and Sam wasn't about to enlighten her.

"How sweet of you." Miss P., as Sam and his brothers used to call her, smiled like a Cheshire cat. "Joy's a lovely woman. I just wish we could do something to get her business into that bakery building. Such a shame for the owners to let it sit there empty when it's exactly the right place for her."

The librarian's gaze met his, wide open and innocent looking, yet Sam had the oddest feeling the lady was trying to tell him something.

"Yes, Joy told me her plans for the old bakery."

"A single mom who's been treated badly. Such a shame." Miss P. shook her head, a warning glint sparking in her blue eyes. "It was already difficult for Joy. Now, with her house unusable, I can't fathom how she'll provide for—" She inclined her head toward Cris.

"For the moment, Joy's baking at the log house on the ranch." Sam wasn't going to provide any more details. "Hey, looks like Marty's free. I'd better go talk to him. I won't be long."

"Oh, take your time, dear." Miss P. patted his shoulder the same way she had when he'd been eight, though she had to stand on tiptoe to reach now. "It's so nice to have you back home, dear. How's your father?"

"Thanks. It's good to be home." Sam was surprised by just how wonderful it felt to be back in his hometown. Sunshine had always been the friendliest place he'd known. "Dad's much improved, thanks. Mom texted that they'll probably return on the weekend or maybe before." He glanced at Cris again, but the kid seemed totally enraptured by a toy. "You need me, just yell."

"I'll be fine." She waved him away.

Reassured Cris wouldn't be alone, Sam headed for Marty's office and told him about the rental house. Thankfully the owner of the hardware and building supply store wasn't a man who asked a lot of questions. He listened, took notes and promised he'd do his best to fix it.

"I was hoping to give her an idea of when you could start work," Sam said.

"Not till after the insurance people have cleared it. Besides, we're focused on Christmas here in the store now, Sam." Marty leaned back in his chair and grinned. "There is one good thing about this mishap though."

"Oh?" Sam didn't understand.

"Well, I intended to lay off most of my construction guys a few weeks ago. Not a lot of work around Sunshine in the winter, you know." He chuckled. "Didn't have to, though, because I got some work for them."

"At this time of year?" Sam raised an eyebrow.

"Yup. A while back I got a letter from some lawyer—Braithwaite was his name. He included a big deposit and asked me to get the old bakery building squared away, ready for use. Rush job for premium pay. My guys are going all out. Place hasn't been used in a while, so there was lotsa stuff to fix, mostly easy stuff." Marty scratched his ear. "The bakery's coming along and we'll be finished soon, so I'll have more work for them, thanks to you. I'll do my best to help your lady, Sam. You want me to run out now and take a look at her house?"

"Not yet." After startling at the words *your lady*, Sam began to wonder who'd authorized his lawyer to order work on *his* bakery building and why he didn't know about it. "Insurance first, as you said. I guess they'll let you know when you can start."

"Good. Gives me time to finish the bakery." Marty looked pleased. "Work like this keeps coming in, I should be able to employ my guys all winter. Times have been tough around town. Be nice not to have to lay anyone off."

"Yes, that would be good. Thanks for the info." Sam returned to the play area.

"I don't think Cris will want to leave yet," Miss Partridge told him, tilting her head toward the three kids who had arrived and were happily playing with Cris.

"Suits me. Can you watch him for a bit longer, Miss P.?" he asked.

"You need to do something else? Certainly I'll watch Cris. My pleasure," she cooed, but there was an inquisitive look in her eyes that Sam recalled from the past. "I'm struggling to decide on a new chain that will suit my favorite bird feeder," she explained casually, but he wasn't fooled by her attitude.

Miss Partridge would eventually find out that he owned Joy's house. Since he didn't want to start tongues wagging about him just yet, he'd better try to keep a low profile. Maybe doing so would put a stop to the ugliest emails he'd read, which Sam was pretty sure came from two local guys who'd always been troublemakers.

"Thanks, Miss P. Marty says he's been refitting the bakery building. Thought I'd go and take a look at what he's doing. I won't be long." Sam walked down the street and stopped in front of the bakery.

Some townsfolk had gathered and were watching

workmen come and go as they speculated about who would move in. Several people greeted Sam by name. Two former school buddies shot him malevolent glares, barely nodding when he said hello.

Curiosity growing, Sam walked around the block, trying to see exactly what was being done. But despite his best efforts at sweet-talking, the foreman wouldn't allow him inside. So he returned to the store to get Cris.

"Did you see what you need to?" Miss Partridge pulled on her purple beret and buttoned her matching coat. "It must be important."

"Just curious. Thank you for helping out." Sam kept his tone blasé. "We have to go now, Cris," he told the boy, who looked disappointed but didn't argue. To distract him, Sam said, "Some of your toys got ruined when the tree fell in the storm. Would you mind helping me pick out new ones for Josh and Becca?"

"Sure." Cris paused in zipping his coat. "An' for me, too?" he asked hopefully.

"And you, for sure," he agreed with a chuckle. "But we have to hurry. Your mom needs those groceries we bought."

"'Kay." Cris went to study the toys.

"So you're buying groceries for Joy?" Miss P.'s eyes widened. "And watching her son. How, er, neighborly." She studied Cris, smiling when he picked out a smaller version of the same truck he'd been playing with for himself and a stick-thin doll with fancy clothes and blond hair for Becca.

"Good choices, Cris. But what about for Josh?" Sam prompted him.

"I dunno," the boy said with a sigh. "He's hard."

"Well, what does he like to do best of all?" Sam grimaced when he noticed the time. Joy would wonder what was taking so long.

"Josh likes to play with wood an' read science stuff." Cris made a face.

"Reading. Just my field. As the town's former librarian, I do know books." Miss Partridge led Cris and Sam toward the bookshelves and selected several titles appropriate for Josh's age. "Any of these would interest him, I think."

"Choose two, Cris," Sam directed. "Thank you very much for your help, Miss Partridge."

"No problem. It's nice to see you buying Joy's children gifts before Christmas," she said in an insinuating tone that annoyed him because it implied something more familiar than mere friendliness.

"Theirs got ruined last night," Sam now felt compelled to explain.

"So you said, dear." She smiled, patted his shoulder again in that genial way that made him nervous, then waved and left.

With the purchases paid for, he and Cris were finally back on the road to the ranch. Sam felt he could breathe again, but he knew sooner or later the truth about him being a property owner in Sunshine would come out. Hopefully not for a while. People already thought poorly of him. If they knew he'd been buying buildings when businesses had gone broke, they'd probably be furious.

"Thank you for the truck," Cris said, one hand resting on his toy as if fearing he'd be asked to return it.

"You're welcome. So what do you want for Christmas?" Sam asked, trying to make conversation.

"Not s'posed to say," Cris told him solemnly.

"Why not?" Was it too extravagant, Sam wondered? Too expensive?

"'Cause. Mom says I can't have it anyway."

"Sometimes moms have to say that." Sam knew he shouldn't, but he couldn't stop himself from asking, "You can tell me though, can't you?"

"No. Because you can't get it for me. Only God can." Cris crossed his arms over his thin chest and stared out the window, leaving Sam to speculate all kinds of things.

Mostly he wondered what a four-year-old kid could possibly want that a loving mom like Joy would refuse to get for him.

Chapter Three

"I did it!" Joy could barely contain her excitement. "I've filled every order and I did it *before* the kids are home from school. Thank You, Lord. And Sam," she added.

But how can I deliver them?

A familiar knuckle rap thudded against the door. Cris beat her to answer then yelled, "Sam's here!"

As if she wouldn't know Sam was in the room the moment he entered. Sam had something—a presence, she supposed it was called. Larger than life. Not like he showed off, but you just knew when he walked in that he was there. At least Joy did. Each time the handsome reporter appeared, her heart picked up its pace and her skin prickled with awareness. Why that should happen wasn't exactly clear.

"Sure smells good in here." Sam sniffed appreciatively. "Need some help loading those orders?"

"Loading?" She frowned, confused.

"Oh. I just assumed you'd have to deliver your baking," he said with a shrug. "I guess folks are picking their orders up here?"

"No, I *do* have to deliver them. But I don't have a vehicle, remember?" She bit her lip, finally voicing the only idea she'd had. "There's this woman I know, Miss Partridge. She said if I ever needed anything to call her. I guess I need to—"

"No!"

Joy blinked at the vehemence in Sam's voice. "But I have to—" He didn't let her finish.

"You can use my car. There's lots of room if I fold the seats down." He picked up a stack of boxes filled with shortbread and carried them to the door.

"Wait, Sam." He stopped and looked at her, his eyes wide, questioning. "I can't use your car," she said flatly.

"Because?" He looked so handsome standing there in his cowboy boots, jeans and battered leather jacket. Under his Stetson, one eyebrow rose. "Well? What's the issue, Mrs. Baker?" He grinned at her dour expression.

"The issue is it's *your* car. And it looks brand-new," she sputtered.

"It is." He shrugged. "So?"

"So what if I hit someone or mark it or—"

"It's a car, Joy. It can be replaced or mended or whatever. You do know how to drive?" he added suddenly, brown eyes narrowing.

"Of course I know how to drive. But…" Exasperation at his casual reaction bubbled inside and rendered her speechless for the moment.

"So can I get on with loading up?" Sam tilted his head to one side, his blazing smile making her knees weak. "Isn't freshness the best thing about baking? If I stand here much longer, you'll have to sell it as day-old stuff."

Joy couldn't think of anything to rebut that, and anyway, Sam didn't wait. He turned on his heel and scooted out the door.

"Mommy?" Cris frowned at her. "What's the matter?"

"Nothing, honey. It's just—"

"Don't you want to drive Sam's car? It's a really nice car," he assured her.

"Thank you, Cris." Sam was back, gathering up more boxes. "What's the holdup, Joy?"

"Becca and Josh aren't home from school yet. I'll wait for the bus then take them with me," she told him, relieved to have thought up the excuse so quickly.

"Nonsense. If you get a move on, you can probably be finished your run before they get home." Sam's knee-knocking grin returned. "I'll make sure the kids get an afternoon snack and start their homework, if they have any. Better get going." He left again before she could naysay his suggestion.

"You have to go, Mommy." Cris nodded sagely.

"You're both very bossy," Joy mumbled as she tugged on her coat and gloves.

"I heard that." But Sam's smile said he didn't hold it against her. "If you bring those two boxes, that's the last of it. You're all ready to go."

"Do you actually have any experience looking after children?" She studied his face, hoping to discern if he was telling the truth.

"I love kids! I looked after Cris okay this morning, didn't I?" Sam had brushed off her earlier comment when Cris had told her about being left in the toy department. "He had Miss Partridge right there. Nobody would dare interfere with her. Now, you'd better be off." He held out the keys. "You have your cell phone? Good. Call if you need anything. Oh, can Cris and I have those left-over cookies?"

"You have to share with Josh and Becca." She smirked when he frowned. "Sharing is an important skill to master," she said with a perfectly straight face.

"Bye, Joy." Sam held the door, waiting.

She couldn't think of another excuse. Besides, she'd promised most of her clients delivery before four o'clock. She had to go. Now.

"You behave," she said to Cris. He nodded. "Thank you," she said to Sam. "I really appreciate this. I will find a way to repay you."

"Cookies," he said with a lazy smile. "Or cake. Or pie. Cinnamon rolls…"

Joy laughed and walked out the door, suddenly aware that she felt more carefree than she had in months, and that was in spite of having just lost her home and her vehicle! She drove slowly out of the yard and turned onto the road toward Sunshine.

"Thank you, God, for sending Sam. He's a real blessing." Then Joy forced her mind off the hunky reporter. Since Nick had died, she'd deliberately kept her brain from noticing any men.

Keep it that way, Mrs. Baker! That was not going to be an easy thing to do, especially now that her brain had adopted his nickname for her.

Two hours later Joy pulled up in front of Miss Partridge's neat white bungalow. This was her last delivery. She sat a moment and just savored the scene before her—perfectly hung Christmas lights in a perfectly decorated yard with big, festive, perfect red bows attached to the lamp stands, a bright red doormat that said *Welcome!* and a perfect giant wreath on the front door that wished *Merry Christmas*.

A sudden longing filled Joy. What would it be like to own her own little home with a garden she could putter in and a porch swing to relax on? How would it feel to hang as many Christmas lights as she wanted and know that even if she left them on all night, she could still afford to pay the power bill at the end of the month?

Miss Partridge generously ordered some of Joy's baking every week, though it seemed as if she gave a lot of it away. Visiting with this woman was a treat, mostly because the lady's spiritual guidance had helped so much when Joy first became a Christian. Now Miss Partridge texted a new verse for her to learn every week.

Joy touched the doorbell, smiling automatically when the door immediately opened.

"'Blessed are the peacemakers: for they shall be called the children of God,'" Joy recited.

"You've got it! My dear Joy, do come in. I've just put on the kettle. Are these my tiny tarts?" The lady closed the door before lifting the box lid to gaze at the colorful array of tarts inside. "How perfect they are. You must have spent hours on these. Shall we taste two with our tea? I don't think my ladies' quilting group will notice them missing."

"A Christmas quilt, isn't it? I heard you're raffling it to raise funds." Joy shrugged off her coat, slipped out of her boots and sat down at the kitchen table. The house was just as pretty inside as out. "You have a beautiful home, Miss Partridge."

"Thank you, dear, but I keep telling you. Please call me Grace." She poured tea for them both, set two tarts on flowered china plates and laid a gauzy napkin by each cup. "There we are. Now, how are you managing, Joy? I met Sam at the hardware store and he mentioned your mishap in passing. What actually occurred?"

"A tree fell on the house. I'm very grateful Sam came along when he did." Joy had the sense her friend wasn't listening. "Is something wrong, Miss—ah, Grace?"

"Well, yes, actually there is. I've just had the worst

news." Grace sipped her tea then sighed. "You're new in town so you wouldn't know this. Every year Sunshine holds a potluck in our community hall on Christmas Eve. Everyone is welcome. It's a gathering time to wish others in our little community a Merry Christmas before the church service."

"It sounds wonderful." Joy knew from Grace's expression there was more to the story.

"It's an old tradition here, much loved," she added sadly. "It's also one that will apparently end this year because the heating system in the hall has an issue and there aren't enough funds to replace it."

"Oh. That's too bad," Joy sympathized quietly. "What can be done?"

"It's truly horrible." Grace sighed and shook her head. "Ordinarily we'd hold some kind of town fundraiser, but this community isn't wealthy and the past year has been a very tough one for many of our ranchers and farmers."

"Yes, I've heard families are feeling the strain," Joy murmured.

"With everyone trying to make a happy Christmas for their own loved ones, the mayor feels it wouldn't be fair to increase taxes to pay for hall repairs, and we don't have a reserve fund to cover the expenses." Miss Partridge played with her tart. "I doubt we could raise enough before Christmas Eve with bingos or the like anyway. But Joy, that hall is the heartbeat of this community. Everything happens there. It joins us together. Now they'll probably have to close it up. That's so sad."

"Yes, it is." Joy didn't know what to do. She tried to change the subject, but that didn't help lift the mood, so she tried a new tactic. "'Have I not commanded thee? Be strong and of a good courage; be not afraid, neither be thou dismayed: for the Lord thy God is with thee whith- ersoever thou goest.'"

But for the first time since Joy had met this woman, quoting a Scripture verse didn't bring a smile to the lady's lips. Miss Partridge seemed truly discouraged. Joy was at a loss as to how to help.

After twenty minutes she rose.

"I'd better get going. The kids will be home and want- ing supper."

"Of course, dear." Grace stood, waiting while Joy donned her hat and boots. "Thank you for the tarts. They're perfect and so delicious," she said, though hers remained untasted on the plate beside her teacup. "Have you heard any more about renting the bakery?"

"No. Whoever owns Possibilities is keeping quiet." Now Joy felt discouraged.

"Well, the Lord is on it, dear. He'll work it out for you," Miss Partridge insisted. "Remember those verses I gave you? 'All things work together for good to them that love God, to them who are called according to His purpose.' They are promises that He will care for you, Joy."

"I've been repeating that one every day. Faith seems so easy with you as my teacher," she said truthfully.

"Believing in God *is* easy." Miss Partridge handed over the cash for her baking. "It's learning to trust Him always, with every detail, that challenges us. That takes time to learn. I'm still learning it myself and I've been His child for many, many years." At last, a bit of the gloom seemed to lift from her face. "Thank you for de- livering these, dear. Do let me know if I can help you in any way."

"Thank you. For everything." Impulsively, Joy leaned forward and hugged the woman, and after only momen- tary hesitation, she received a hug in return. "Bye now."

"Pray about the community center, will you?" Miss Partridge asked quietly. "Sunshine surely does need His help now. Bye, dear."

By the time Joy had picked up more baking supplies, it was far later than she'd intended and darkness had fallen. She drove back to the ranch carefully, apprehensive about stray wildlife and possibly damaging Sam's car. But she forgot all about that the moment she entered the yard site.

The exterior of the little log house now glowed as brightly as the main house, with Christmas lights resembling crystal icicles hanging from the eaves. The shrubbery on one side of the stairs twinkled with fat, round red bulbs that made her think of holly berries. A massive lighted spruce wreath graced the front door.

It looked so lovely. Joy stood by the car just taking it in. She stared for such a long time that the kids came running, demanding to know if she liked it.

"It's wonderful," she whispered. "So pretty. Did you help with this?"

"Yes. Come see what else we did, Mom." Josh's face glowed, alight with excitement. "Sam's helping us."

"Welcome home, Joy." Her heart did the familiar bump and flutter when Sam appeared, that famous smile stretching his lips. He took the grocery bags out of the vehicle, handing one to each child, but reserving the heaviest for himself. "Let's put these inside the door, guys, then we can show your mom our creations."

That's when Joy spied a massive snowman standing on one side of the front yard and a half-finished snow fort on the other. "Wow! Those are both huge."

"Aren't they great?" Josh looked more excited than she'd seen him in ages. "Sam's showing us how he and his brothers made a fort just like this when they were kids.

An' we got lots to do yet. Come on, Becca and Cris. Let's put these bags in the house so we can finish."

Her children dashed to the house, bounded up the stairs and set the bags of supplies inside so fast, Joy feared for her eggs. Then with a whoop and a holler, they returned to packing snow onto an igloo-like shape.

"C'mon, Sam!" Cris called.

"Be there in a sec." Sam walked beside Joy to the house, and when she was inside he handed her his grocery bag.

"Thank you so much for watching them," she said. "And for doing all this with them. They've always wanted to decorate outside." *But I could never afford that.*

"Why don't you come and join us? It should be a family fort." His grin set her heart racing again. "You know you want to."

"I need to put these away and—" Joy paused, thought a moment. How often did she get a chance to just play with her kids? This was a rare opportunity not to be missed. "Okay, I will. For a few minutes. Then I'll start supper."

"It's already in the slow cooker. Soup." He chuckled at her expression. "I told you I can cook. Don't worry. The kids and I cleaned up our mess."

"It's very kind of you," she began, but he shook his head.

"Come on, before it's too dark to see anything." Then he was gone, rushing out the door as if he *wanted* to help her three fatherless kids build a snow fort on a winter's evening.

Sam Calhoun was like no other man Joy had ever met. She grabbed her gloves and hurried out to join them.

Chapter Four

"The community center, huh?" Later that evening Sam leaned his elbows on the table and cupped his chin in his palms, glad the kids were in bed so they could discuss this.

"It sounded as if it's pretty bad," Joy told him.

"Our family has spent so many fun Christmas potlucks in that hall over the years. It seems wrong to cancel it." He smiled at the recollections. "Do you know that supper is the only Christmas event some folks in Sunshine ever attend?"

"It is?" She frowned. "Why?"

"We have some very hard-up folks around here," he explained. "But at the Christmas potluck they can bring a jar of pickles if they want, and nobody notices or cares if that's all they bring. Everyone knows there will be oodles left over." He fiddled with a place mat. "It's not just the food, it's the friendship and the joy that we all share at our Christmas potluck."

"Grace said it's been a really tough year for Sunshine," Joy said thoughtfully. "I heard someone at the grocery store mention there was even some question at the last council meeting about bothering to put up the Christmas angels on the streetlights. Apparently the wiring's old and not functioning properly. With the economy here suffering, the atmosphere in town feels almost depressed."

"Depressed? Before Christmas? That's pretty grim, isn't it?" A wave of sadness swooped over Sam. Was that how his first Christmas at home in years would be? Grim?

"It's sure not a fun place at the moment, and I doubt that heating system problem is helping." Joy's gorgeous eyes held shadows. "Grace seemed really down about it. She said the mayor feels it would be wrong to ask for donations to repair the heating, if it even can be repaired, when lots of folks are already struggling just to provide Christmas for their family." Joy's sigh for people she barely knew touched him. "I'd donate baking if someone organized a fundraising event, but—"

"Fundraising! That's it." Sam sat up straight as ideas began to bloom inside his head.

"A bake sale?" she said dubiously, her nose wrinkling. "I don't think that will—"

"Not *a* fundraiser." Sam wondered if it could actually work. "We need an entire event of fundraisers. Maybe several," he said thoughtfully.

"But I just told you, nobody can—"

"Not to get money from the townsfolk. Something else, something bigger..." Scenes from his past, on a lonely Christmas Eve, in a small northern European town, swam into focus.

"Sam?" He blinked back to awareness to find Joy staring at him, a worried frown on her face. "You kind of blanked out just now, and you did the same thing this morning. Are you okay?"

"I'm fine," he assured her absently as pictures flashed through his mind. "The town needs to hold a festival. The Twelve Days of Christmas Festival."

"Um, okay. Good idea," she said cautiously.

"I hear a *but*." He glared at her. "Well?"

"But," she said emphatically, her eyes snapping emerald sparks at him, "the twelve days of Christmas actually start *on* Christmas Day and run to January 6, which would be too late for the hall," she reminded him. "The days *before* Christmas are called Advent."

"That's perfect!" Sam felt as if new life filled his lungs. This was something he could help with that wouldn't bring up his past. And it would give him something to do while he waited for news that his career sacrifice had been worth it.

You weren't going to get involved, remember? Getting too involved is what cost you your career and forced you to come back to the ranch.

Sam put a lid on that voice. "We'll call it the Advent Festival."

"Ah." Joy studied him for several minutes, green eyes cloudy. "What exactly happens at this Advent Festival?" She sounded wary.

"Not exactly sure. Hear me out." He inhaled and began his story. "Three years ago, I was in this little town in Poland. A lot of poor people lived there, and they didn't have much money to celebrate Christmas in their broken-down church. Their priest wanted to help them, so he organized a festival to draw in folks from other communities. That festival was so successful they raised enough money to refurbish their church, so they held a Christmas Day service in it for themselves and anyone else who wanted to come. They handed out bags of groceries so everyone could celebrate the birth of Christ."

"How wonderful! I wish I'd seen that." Joy stared at him. He knew ideas were filling her head just as he felt them gathering inside him. "So you're thinking vendor stalls?" she asked.

"Well, yes, because people always want to shop for unique Christmas gifts. We'd encourage that, of course. Also, we'd need stops along the way where folks could get a drink or a snack, yet still be part of whatever the activity is."

"But you're thinking more than that?" She studied him curiously.

"Way more," Sam confirmed.

"Such as?"

"Events. Lots of events," he emphasized while noting the way the firelight turned Joy's hair a pale claret hue. *Focus, Calhoun.*

"Explain." She grabbed a pad and a pen and waited.

"Contests. Maybe snowman building one day, games on a little open-air rink in the town square another. An evening talent show. Hot-chocolate-making contests for the kids. Live theater." The concepts came so fast and hard he struggled to rattle them off slowly enough so she could write them down.

"All amazing, though not exactly unusual. Next." She cheered encouragingly, her pen flying.

"We don't need them all to be unusual, but we do need them to be fun and maybe just a little different from the norm."

"Yes." She paused then, her huge grin dimming. "It's risky, though. What if the weather turns awful? There's no indoor place in town where we could host things. What if we don't raise enough to pay for the hall repairs before Christmas Eve? And even if we do, what if we don't have enough time to get it fixed before the potluck?"

She made good points. Sam thought hard for several moments.

"The only way to do this successfully is for council to get a loan to pay for the repairs," he insisted. "Then we could use the community center for some of the events for our Advent Festival. We could even schedule more than one thing at the same time and we could repeat events on different days so that no one would have to miss any event they wanted to be part of."

"Keep going," she encouraged, as if she knew his head whirled with possibilities.

"Well, that hall is right in the center of town. It could be the focal point, Christmas central. It would also keep our guests in Sunshine's commercial hub so businesses would get maximum exposure, and hopefully that would increase their sales. If we do it right, maybe this year Sunshine won't have any *going-out-of-business sales* after the New Year." Possibilities grew in Sam's brain.

"What about the loan?" Joy asked.

"We could pay it back with the proceeds of the festival," he said.

"We'll need a lot of proceeds, Sam. Miss Partridge said it was a big bill." Joy related what Grace had told her about the estimate for repairs. "Are you sure the town would agree to such a large loan? Could Sunshine bring in that much before Christmas? Can they pay it off without having it hang over the town for years to come? That's what everyone will be asking."

He liked Joy's businesslike approach. She, unlike him, didn't get totally swept away by grandiose ideas. She'd be a great asset to the town's businesses.

"I can't guarantee anything, Joy. No one can," Sam said quietly. "But if we don't do something, if Sunshine doesn't have its community center, I can almost guarantee that our town will die away, just like the other small towns around here have done. That community center is the core of Sunshine."

"Okay. Let's think about it tonight," Joy suggested. "If it still seems viable in the morning, maybe you should meet with town officials and suggest a town meeting. A big plan like this is going to need everyone on board to be successful."

"Good idea. Besides, you need to get some sleep." Sam rose and pulled on his coat. As he did, he heard a crackle and was reminded of something. "Oh, I forgot. Drew gave me this letter for you. Apparently someone hand-delivered it this afternoon." He tugged the plain white envelope out of his pocket and gave it to her.

"Who knows I'm here?" He watched Joy study the envelope on which only her name was neatly printed. No return address. She shrugged, slit it open with one fingernail and then read the words. Her expression changed to shock then astonishment. She frowned and reread the letter, as if she couldn't quite process what it said.

"Is it bad news?" Sam held his breath. *She's already dealing with so much, Lord.*

"On the contrary." Joy lifted her curly head, her eyes suddenly awash with tears. "It's the very best news. That company, Possibilities, has agreed to rent me the bakery building *for the amount I suggested* in my offer to them. I'm to take a look inside on Thursday afternoon, when the repairs will be complete. If I decide I still want it, I can move in on Friday." She gaped at him. "Sam, today's Tuesday. That's only three days away. Three days!"

"I heard they'd been doing renovations there. Great." He'd glimpsed his lawyer's name on the letterhead, but he wasn't going to mention that. He had to text his dad first. Ben was the only one who could have set this in motion and his timing couldn't have been better. "How will you get in?"

"It says to contact Marty at the hardware store." Joy gazed at the letter as if overwhelmed. "Move in Friday? I have two big party orders for Saturday. Preparing them with so much space would be amazing." She glanced up, her face blazing with happiness, eyes shining with unshed tears. "Miss Partridge was right. God does have His eye on me. What a tremendous answer to prayer."

"I'm so happy for you, Joy." Sam wanted to hug her, to comfort her, to let her know he supported her. But all of those actions meant risking romantic involvement and he couldn't, wouldn't ever let that happen again. Once burned, twice shy.

"I'm happy for me, too," she whispered and smiled when Sam laughed.

"I'd better go home," he said. "It's late. Good night."

"Good night, Sam. And thank you. For the soup and decorating with the kids, and the snow fort and your car and...everything."

The way Joy looked at him, her curls turning that reddish gold in the light as they swirled around her beautiful face, made his heart race. *Get out of here, man. Now!*

"You're very welcome, Joy." Sam quietly closed the door behind him and walked through the softly falling snow to his parents' house. He paused on the doorstep and gazed around.

It felt right to be here on the Double H, to help out with the odd trail ride on the ranch, to pitch in wherever he was needed, even in town, if they'd let him. He'd gladly help Joy move into the bakery building, would even rope his brothers into helping her. Dreaming up ideas for a festival was something he could help with, too.

But there had to be more if God wanted him to stay here. Sam needed permanent work he could do, something that would fulfill him as much as reporting had.

But what?

Long-term, Sam had no plans. He was waiting for God's direction. Anyway, he could do nothing, make no future decisions, until that business in the Middle East was settled. It wasn't his reputation he wanted restored, though that would be nice. He was waiting for a message: the knowledge that his lie had been worth it, that lives had been saved.

His fingers closed around the burner phone in his pocket that he carried everywhere since it had been handed to him when he'd first deplaned in New York. But it was still silent.

Okay, then, while he waited for vindication, he'd maintain the secrecy he'd clung to for this long. Meanwhile, he'd do whatever he could to help here. He'd approach town council tomorrow and float his idea for the festival. Sam knew some would naysay it just because it came from him. There was still a lot of animosity toward him because of that false report he'd filed.

If only— No! He'd done it and he'd do it again if needed. There was no going back. There was only going forward. He intended to do that just as soon as he found out his sacrifice had been successful.

Only he wasn't sure what he'd be going forward to. Asking God didn't help. He couldn't seem to break through the spiritual silence that had fallen on him the day he'd illegally crossed that border in the Middle East.

But Sam was here now, so he'd try to make a difference, because Sunshine was *his* hometown. Also because he'd made himself a vow many years ago to do whatever he could to keep the little town that he loved alive.

The following evening, Joy stood at the back of the boardroom in the town offices, a little surprised by how many people had shown up for this quickly called town meeting. She was glad everyone would get to hear Sam put forward his ideas. But when she'd asked Kira to baby-sit so she could attend, she'd had no idea that what she'd hear from these townspeople would be so negative.

"You're all gung ho for council to take on this big loan, Sam. But Sunshine is barely scraping by. We can't afford more debt. Though I don't suppose you, with all your hotshot globe-trotting—which someone else paid for, by the way—would understand that." Evan Smith sneered.

"I think you know that I've seen plenty of poverty worldwide, Evan," Sam responded, his voice calm, even relaxed. "And I do understand that it's a leap for Sunshine to risk so much money when there are other pressing needs. But what's the alternative? Sit back and let the hall deteriorate so it's never usable?"

The glum faces in the room testified to how little anyone wanted that.

"Sometimes you have to take a giant step of faith to get a reward. What I'm proposing is a way to have the community center available for the Christmas Eve pot-luck and also recoup the expense for fixing it *while* we use it." Sam's brown eyes probed the crowd. "A town-wide festival could bring in a lot of customers for our businesses, if we do it right."

"Who's gonna show us how to do it right?" a spectator called out scornfully. "You? Like you did with that lying report you gave?"

How could Sam keep his cool? How could he look

so unaffected? Indignant that anyone would condemn the very person who was trying to help, Joy cleared her throat and rose.

"Maybe we can't do this," she said quietly, and then challenged, "But maybe we can. Is it so impossible for us to just listen to Sam's ideas?" She kept her voice firm, her comments focused. "The community center is very important to Sunshine and its residents. If there *is* some way to get it functioning again, shouldn't we at least hear about it before putting down the idea and the person suggesting a solution?"

"What's it to you?" Mr. Smith asked. "You're not part of our town."

"I have been for the past three months," she informed him in a crisp tone. "Beginning Friday, I'm relocating my bakery business in town." Joy felt immense satisfaction at putting him in his place, though she had yet to actually inspect the building or give her acceptance to Possibilities. Still, as Miss Partridge would say, *When God opens a door, walk through it.* "We'll be open Saturday morning," she added bravely.

Many who'd already used her baking services called out their congratulations, as did the mayor. After thanking them, Joy continued.

"As a small business in Sunshine, I'm very interested in hearing about anything that will help generate additional income and increase my bottom line. As a business owner, I can't imagine why you wouldn't be, too, Mr. Smith."

Murmurs of assent filled the room. The mayor invited Sam to proceed with his ideas, which he did with colorful photos. Joy figured he must have taken them in that place in Poland, during the festival he'd told her about.

By the end of his presentation, the mood in the room was definitely positive, even festive.

"I say we get that loan to fix the hall and give Sam's idea a try. Call for the vote, Mayor," Councilor Partridge called.

It had come as a surprise to Joy that Miss Partridge had been recently elected to council, but then the former librarian seemed to have her fingers in most everything that happened in Sunshine.

"The ayes win it, five votes to two," Mayor Brown declared after council had voted. "The town of Sunshine will take out a loan to repair the community center and repay it with funds derived from our Advent Festival."

Excitement rose in the room until one angry voice cut through.

"And when this dumb idea fails and taxpayers are left holding this loan?" Evan Smith demanded. "Is Sam Calhoun going to foot the bill and pay it off?"

Silence reigned.

Then to Joy's utter disbelief, Sam answered.

"Yes, Evan, if we don't generate enough with the festival, I will cover the loan myself. You have my word."

Everyone gaped until Evan scoffed, "Because your word is so trustworthy, isn't it, Sam?"

The mayor called the meeting back to order, reprimanded Councilman Smith for his rudeness and thanked Sam for backing the loan. Then Marty from the hardware store asked to be heard.

"I nominate Sam to spearhead our festival. He has all the ideas—good ones, too, I might add." The man grinned at Sam as if he was a coconspirator. "Sam is doing this out of the goodness of his heart. He doesn't have a vested interest like the rest of us do. All he wants is for the town to have a hall, and he's got the smarts to help get ours fixed. So I say we put him in charge of getting that done."

Immediately a group began chanting "Sam" until the mayor called for order.

"Well, what do you say, Sam? Will you take the lead on our Advent Festival?"

Sam rose, pretend glared at Marty and then shrugged.

"Guess I can hardly say no now, can I?" He extended his arm, palms up. "Okay, I'll be your lead guy. But I'm going to need a lot of hands-on help, *your* hands, to make it happen. This is going to be a community effort and we'll start tomorrow evening. We have to get this thing planned and advertised if we're going to pull off an event every day before Christmas. Do I have your help?"

Joy silently applauded as someone immediately asked for a sign-up sheet. While it circulated, smiles abounded and laughter echoed in the room. It was the sound of hope, she thought. And Sam had made it happen.

Twenty minutes later Miss Partridge requested the meeting be adjourned. Joy remained in the background, watching as folks clapped Sam on the shoulder and offered their help. Only a few crept away without speaking to anyone. Two men conferred in a corner with Evan Smith, whispering, their faces furious.

All Joy could think was *Sam better be careful. Those three are trouble.*

"It's not going to be easy, is it?" Joy said as she rode home with Sam.

"Nope." Sam shrugged, pretending unconcern. "It's a huge undertaking and some don't trust me. I have to earn their trust. That's okay. I can do that as long as they don't shut me down before we give this a chance." At least he hoped he could.

"I'll help whenever and however I can," Joy promised.

How generous she was! As if she didn't have enough of her own issues going on. Sam admired this woman more every time they were together.

"Are you ready to check out the bakery tomorrow and move in on Friday?" he asked.

"Yes. Tomorrow at five I'll tour it, make sure everything is okay. Grace Partridge suggested I hire Clara Ens as my baker. She was head baker for the former owners, and Grace says she's the only thing that kept them open as long as they were."

"Sounds like Clara will be a real asset," he said. "I don't know her well, but if Miss Partridge recommended her, that's worth a lot."

"That's what I thought." Joy grinned. "So I hired her. On Friday we'll bake our orders in the cabin while the kids are at school. Clara will deliver them while I haul stuff to the bakery. Then we'll get everything set up and prepare for opening on Saturday morning."

Sam was a little bothered that he hadn't had time to go through the bakery and make sure the place was up to snuff. He'd always insisted that safety checks be done on his properties before anyone moved in. Since his dad insisted Marty had already done that, Sam would just have to trust.

But he couldn't help asking, "You're sure the place will be okay?"

"God sent it, so it has to be." Joy grinned. "I'm pressing on with my plans and I'm nervous enough. Don't dampen my excitement."

"No way," Sam reassured her. "I'm on your side."

"There's supposed to be a truck coming with fresh supplies at six on Friday evening, and another in the morning with fresh bread." Joy frowned. "According to Clara, the ovens aren't big enough to bake any more than the artisan breads and all the specialty products I want to sell. She suggested I bring in regular sliced bread, just as the former owners did, though she says it's not the best quality."

"That doesn't sound good." Sam frowned.

"It isn't the best, but it's what I have to do. For now. Ideally, I'd prefer to find another smaller bakery to supply me, one that focuses on quality and not mass production, but I guess that's part of my future plan." She paused then asked hesitantly, "Can I borrow your car again on Friday to move, Sam?"

"Sure, but you won't need it." He grinned at her double take.

"Why won't I?"

"Because Drew, Zac and I will put everything you need in the ranch's trailer and deliver it to your bakery." He brushed off her thanks. "Once you're moved in, you can take a look at a used van."

"I can't afford to buy a van, Sam," Joy gasped. "Not along with everything else."

"You'll need it for business deliveries and for transportation. Anyway, I think you can't afford *not* to buy the one I'm thinking of." He chuckled at her blink of surprise. "At least you're not naysaying me. I like that."

"Humph!" Joy crossed her arms and waited for an explanation.

"You look nothing like my former fiancée, Joy. But you show the same pluck and grittiness Celia always had, no matter what hot spot I asked her to film." He was surprised by the memory, yet so not willing to go back to that other dark era of his life.

"Fiancée? Film?" Joy was obviously confused.

"I keep forgetting you're new to Sunshine. Celia was my fiancée and also my camerawoman on a number of assignments," Sam explained. He hated having to say it, but he owed her honesty. "Celia lost her life because of me."

"I doubt that, but tell me the rest of it," Joy ordered.

She listened, her face revealing her chagrin as he explained the intense exposé he'd done on an infamous drug lord after months of verifying his story, and how Celia had been kidnapped in retaliation.

"I pressed too hard. That's why they took her. Retribution. But they didn't realize she had a severe allergy." Sam licked his lips and tried to swallow. He'd never been able to assuage his guilt. "Celia died while in captivity because they withheld her inhaler."

"That wasn't your fault, Sam. It was the kidnappers' fault." Joy tilted her head to one side and studied him. "Anyway, I doubt Celia would have gone with you if she hadn't wanted to. She loved you. She would have wanted to be with you, share your world."

"That's kind of you to say." Celia had loved him, and Sam had loved her. He should have protected her. The agony of those days still hung over him like a cloud. That was one reason he'd blocked love from his life. He couldn't go through that grief again.

"I'm sure it's true," Joy insisted. After a moment she murmured, "Now, what was it you were saying about this van?"

"I knew you wouldn't be able to resist." Sam burst out laughing, though it took effort for him to let go of the pain-filled past. "It's Mr. Porter's. He's moving into the nursing home. He can't drive anymore because of vision problems."

"Oh." Her lovely green eyes clouded over. "That's sad."

"It is," Sam agreed. "Mr. Porter is one of Sunshine's most generous citizens. He turned over his house, lock, stock and barrel, free and clear, to a young family who just had theirs repossessed. He told Zac yesterday that he wants to find someone who will use and enjoy his van as much as he has. Someone who needs it. That's you!"

"I can't afford it," she reiterated. Sam named the price. He laughed when she argued, "That can't be right!"

"It's not a mistake," he promised. "Mr. Porter asked Zac to check around, see who could put it to good use. Zac thinks the van would be perfect for you and the kids because it's only three years old. Anyway, Mr. Porter doesn't have any family. He has to sell it to someone, so why not you?"

Sam had never enjoyed anyone's happiness as much as he did Joy's. She seemed so thrilled with everything, small and large.

He really liked this woman, but only as a friend. Celia's loss still haunted him. He would never go through that again. Never.

Joy didn't make snap decisions, not since long ago, when since she'd finally realized just how difficult it was to fix the problems that resulted from the impulsive choices she'd made then.

But with her car out of commission permanently, she needed a vehicle. Badly. This van would be perfect for deliveries, and the incredible price was just about manageable on her small budget, if she used some of her carefully hoarded savings and a portion of the tiny operating loan she'd taken out.

"I'll take it," she told Sam in a breathless rush.

"Great." He winked at her. "Can I confess something?"

"That sounds ominous." She frowned at him. "What?"

"I already told Zac you wanted it." He wrinkled his nose as if he was waiting for her to blast him.

"Thank you." How could she berate him for snapping up a deal like that? "I can only afford it because I learned today that my car's being written off. That insurance money will help a lot. Besides, I can't keep driving yours."

"A businesswoman needs her own wheels," he agreed. "Mr. Porter wants to have it serviced and checked over to make sure everything's working perfectly. You'll get it Thursday afternoon."

"It's amazing," she whispered.

"The van?" Sam looked confused.

"My life," she clarified. "I can't believe how everything is coming together. I've prayed so many times for the bakery and appropriate transportation and then suddenly—whoosh! It arrives all at once." She couldn't stifle a giggle of relief.

"I guess that's how God answers prayer sometimes, though I don't think it's ever happened to me like that." Sam suddenly sounded sober and Joy remembered the town meeting.

"I'm sorry that Evan Smith was so horrible," Joy murmured. "Especially when you're underwriting the loan and volunteering to run the festival and you don't even live in Sunshine anymore."

"I think I'll be here for a while," Sam said very quietly. "I don't have anywhere else to go. But really, it's okay, Joy. Don't worry about Evan. He's always had a nasty streak. That's nothing new. Anyway, I know a lot of people don't trust me now," he admitted.

"Because of that story. Does it bother you, all the negativity?" she asked and then wondered if she should have voiced that.

"Of course it bothers me," he said, his tone irritated. "But in the same situation, I'd do it again, so I have no regrets."

Joy didn't understand that at all, but she could hardly

press him on it. He pulled up in front of the log house and shifted into Park before he spoke again.

"I came home wanting to do something while I wait, something that will make a difference." Sam's big, generous smile was back. "Running a festival should certainly do that."

"No kidding," she said, admiring his courage.

"It'll be a challenge." His grin widened. "Good thing I love challenges."

"I hope it works out." *Because I don't want you to face another mistake.* "Thanks for the ride. Good night, Sam."

After Joy paid Kira and checked on the kids, she stood alone in the center of the log house while a thousand questions fought each other in her brain. Primarily, she wondered how it could be that everything in her world had started coming together with Sam's arrival?

Equally as curious, Sam had said that fake story bothered him. Yet he'd also said that given the chance he'd release it again. And that he was waiting. What did it all mean?

A chiming clock alerted Joy to the time. She quickly changed clothes before she began assembling ingredients for tomorrow's order of cinnamon rolls. But her brain had even more questions.

Like why had Sam backed that loan? Was he so wealthy that it didn't matter? And how on earth was it possible to bring in enough cash to cover it in such a short time?

Joy did not want him to fail.

And therein lay the most important question. Why was Sam's success so important to her when he was almost a stranger?

Chapter Five

"Sam, you shouldn't have promised to cover that loan." Drew shook his head at his brother over his steaming coffee cup later that evening as they lounged in their parents' living room. "What if you can't repay it?"

"Then I'll donate the money." Sam shrugged. "Thanks to you managing my investments, I have enough in reserve."

"Yes, but it would make a big dent." Drew frowned. "You don't owe anyone anything, Sam. The problem with the hall was not of your making."

"Maybe not, but since I'm here, I can help fix it. I intend to go ahead with the festival, and if it doesn't go well, I won't allow people to say the town's on the hook because of me." Sam took a deep breath and tried again to make his family understand. "The community hall is the lifeblood of Sunshine. Remember, that place saw us through Boy Scouts, our teen years, all the special times. It's an icon."

"It's just a hall, bro." Drew sighed when Sam turned to Zac.

"Your wedding shower was there." Sam listed more reminders. "Our graduation parties were there. Everything noteworthy in our lives since we came to the Double H is tied up in that place. Mom and Dad had their wedding reception there." He shrugged. "That hall has history. No way I'm going to stand back and just let it go."

"Yes, but—" Zac groaned when Sam shook his head to stop his objection. He turned to their father who lay sprawled in his easy chair, having arrived home from the hospital earlier than the brothers had expected. "You try to talk reason to him, Dad."

"It's done. No reason to discuss it any further. Let the folks rest." Sam could tell from the tiredness on Ben's face that the long trip home from the hospital couldn't have been easy for him. His mom looked beat, too. "Just be available when I ask for help," he told his brothers. "Especially Friday, because that's when we're going to move Joy's stuff into the bakery building."

"We're always available for you. You know we've got your back." Drew motioned to Zac. "Come on. Might as well go home. You know we never could talk our kid brother out of any of the crazy ideas he always gets about Sunshine. The prosperity of our town has been like his own personal mission for years."

"That's for sure. Once an idea to help Sunshine lodges in Sam's noggin, nothing can change his mind. Wasted effort trying to talk him out of it. Night, Dad. Rest easy. You, too, Ma." Zac followed Drew in hugging the pair. Then they left.

Sam glanced around. Here was a place he could help, too. Good thing he'd already hired two local cleaning ladies to assist his mom. She couldn't argue about it until she found out when they arrived tomorrow, and then it would be too late.

"I'm really glad you two are home, Ma."

"So are we. But what's going on, Sammy?" Bonnie asked. "So much money and you've worked so hard to earn it. Why did you really do this?" Concern was written all over his mom's face.

"Because I have to do something while I'm here. Because I can't just sit around waiting for—" Sam closed his fingers around the burner phone in his pocket, barely able to stop himself from blurting out what he'd promised to keep secret.

"Waiting for...?" Bonnie studied him curiously.

"I can't keep waiting for God to explain what I'm supposed to do next," he quickly revised. "I can't stand the idea that Sunshine will go the way of other towns around here either, slowly dying because nobody will do anything to save it. It's only a community hall that needs some fixing, but everyone in town is too scared to take a risk. So I will. I can always earn more money if I have to."

Oh yeah? the voice in his head mocked. *Doing what?*

"I know the town's success has always been very important to you, son. Supporting your community is a legacy your birth dad impressed on you, and it's truly admirable. But, Sam, it's so much money." Ma's expression made him smile. He doubted Bonnie's motherly concern for her *boys* would ever abate.

"It's thanks to me you're into that bakery for a goodly sum for repairs, painting and rewiring, too." Ben frowned. "I should have waited until you okayed it before I told your lawyer to get things started. Did I mess things up there?"

"Are you kidding? Your timing in rehabbing the place is impeccable. Joy will be the perfect tenant and the place will reopen, just as I wanted when I bought the building. Having our own bakery in town is exactly what we need." Sam grimaced at the way Ben's shoulders seemed to sag with relief. His loved ones had been doing his job for him. Ben already had too much on his plate with the ranch. About time Sam came back and handled his own affairs. Was that what God wanted? "Thanks for taking care of things for me, Dad."

"Sorry about the house, son. I tried to tell you in the emails, but—"

"Forget about it. You did great. Insurance will handle it now." Sam shrugged. "Joy and her kids are better off here at the ranch in the log house anyway. She's got help close by if she needs it while she opens her new business."

"You like her," Bonnie murmured.

"I do. She's smart, capable, determined, and she's got a big heart." He shook his head when his mother's eyes began to glow. "Forget it, Ma. Friendship is all we'll share. Losing Celia, well, that was a game changer for me. I'm not going there again. Anyway, my work sometimes gets risky. I don't want to endanger anyone ever again. That's why I can't get involved."

"Ha! Seems to me you're *really involved,* thanks to this latest scheme of yours." Ben snorted as he studied Sam with an intensity that wouldn't allow prevarication. "Wanna tell us what really happened over there, son?" he asked quietly. "The truth."

Sam rose. How he wished he could pour out the whole story to these loving people and let them share his pain. But it wasn't finished yet. Until he got a text or a call on his burner phone, he couldn't talk about any of it. Not without risking dire consequences for someone else, someone who'd helped Sam and might pay for that with their life.

"I did what I had to do, Dad. That's all there is to it." His kissed his mom's cheek. "I'm glad you're both home safe and sound, though I wish you'd called one of us to come get you." He shook his head at their proud smiles. "You're too stubborn. But I love you anyway. You're tired. You should go to bed. I am."

He had his foot on the bottom stair when his dad's voice stopped him.

"What about you and God, Sam? You got that worked out yet?"

"Not yet, Dad." Sam kept climbing. In his room he pulled the burner phone out of his pocket.

Nothing. No message to tell him all was well, that he could restart his life. Nothing to say that the most horrible time in his entire career had finally ended.

He got into bed, trying to force himself to sleep and failing.

Thing was, it all came down to God. Where was He when Sam had been alone in that dank hole in the Middle East? Why hadn't God answered his prayers? Would God let someone die because of him, because he'd pushed too hard, gone too far?

The sense of abandonment saddened Sam now as it had before. It was the same feeling he'd had when he'd lain in that hospital bed as a kid all those years ago, cowering in pain, misery and fright after learning his parents had been killed in the accident that had injured him and his brothers. The same emptiness that had held him captive after Celia's death.

Sam felt utterly alone.

Then Joy's lovely face swam into his mind. He could hear her voice in his head as she faced Evan.

Is it so impossible for us to just listen to Sam?

Sam appreciated her staunch defense of him, though he wouldn't tell her that. Best not to get too close. Joy couldn't know that he'd set himself a challenge to prove he could make a difference here without a camera or a network to back him, that he'd vowed to show he wasn't utterly useless without his former career. Maybe Sam had lost all credibility with everyone else, but not with himself.

Maybe not with Joy either?

He didn't know why that was so important; he only knew it mattered to him what she thought. It mattered a lot.

"You're absolutely sure this is what you want for your new business?" Sam asked late Thursday afternoon. He traced one finger across a wall as if expecting to find a dust trail, except the entire bakery had been cleaned and repainted.

"Of course." Joy twisted from studying the big display cases to stare at him with surprise. "It's just as perfect as I remembered."

"It doesn't look perfect. The walls are, uh, crooked," he said, wrinkling his nose.

"They go with the floor." Joy looked at him and wondered what was going on. Didn't he want her to have her business here?

"No second thoughts?" He sounded compelled to ensure she truly was satisfied.

"None. This place will suit me perfectly." What was wrong with him? "You seem, er, concerned about something, Sam. Want to tell me what's bugging you?"

Why did she keep getting these feelings that he was hiding something from her?

"I know your business is none of my business," he said sheepishly, apologetically. The way he avoided looking directly at her disconcerted Joy. "But this place isn't fancy. I just want to be certain you don't get in here and then wish you'd waited for something better."

"I won't because there isn't anything that's better in the town of Sunshine. This building is perfect for me, Sam." She ran her hand over the bruised but still very functional butcher-block counter. "I've always thought so."

"Always?" He frowned.

"When I heard this place was closing the first time, I

came here and asked the owners if I could look around."
She smiled at his surprise.

"When was that?"

"Hmm. Before the last owner, I guess. Two years ago?
Maybe a little longer." Wasn't it sweet of Sam to be so
concerned about her? "That day is when my dream to
start my bakery in this building began. So you see, I'm
not rushing into anything. I doubt there's anything about
this place that I haven't thought and rethought from every
angle." She twirled around, feeling childish but not caring. "This is my heart's desire finally coming true."

"Then I'm very happy for you, Joy." Sam waited while
she walked through the bakery one last time. She caught
him surreptitiously glancing at his watch.

"Am I making you late for something?"

"Not late," he corrected. "But if you're finished here
for now, I should get going."

"What's on your agenda this late in the day?" She'd
hardly seen him since that town hall meeting the other
evening, other than to notice he was constantly coming
or going from the ranch in someone else's vehicle since
he'd insisted she use his for deliveries.

"I have an idea for a promotional video for Experience
Christmas, and I need to talk to Miss Partridge about it
before the meeting tonight." He seemed relieved when
she shook off her preoccupation with the bakery to focus
on his words.

"Experience Christmas. That's the name you've given
the festival?" He nodded. "And you need to speak to Miss
Partridge about a video?" Joy couldn't mask her curiosity. "Can I ask why?"

"I want her to star in it." Sam said it so matter-of-factly
that she didn't immediately grasp what he'd said. When
she did, she stopped dead in the middle of what would
soon be her coffee-shop area.

"Sorry? You want Grace Partridge to be in your promotional video?" Joy repeated, trying to form a mental picture of that.

"Yes, I do. She's perfect." Sam grabbed her arm, led her to the door and held it open for her. He waited while she locked it, then walked with her to his car and opened that door for her, as well. "Your new van was delivered to the Double H this afternoon," he said.

"Great." Joy tried to figure out what he meant about the video, but her mind remained blank. She waited for him to get in the driver's seat. "Why her?"

"Why not?" Sam said.

"Well, she's lovely, of course. A wonderful woman and an asset to the community." Joy paused. "But, well—she doesn't exactly scream Hollywood star power…" She frowned, then, so she wouldn't offend, quickly added, "Does she?"

"Grace Partridge is extremely photogenic." Sam grinned. "Besides, she did so much public speaking in her years at the library that she's a natural at communicating. People see that big smile of hers and they feel comfortable. She's exactly what I want."

"Oh." Dumbfounded by this new concept of the town's former librarian, Joy couldn't think of another thing to say. When they arrived at Grace's home, she followed him inside, her curiosity raging.

"You want me to do what?" Miss Partridge appeared as flabbergasted as Joy had felt before Sam explained.

"Make a commercial," he repeated now, as if it was the easiest thing in the world. "You're perfect. If you like, I could show you now what I have in mind. We'd use the town square as the backdrop. Our team has already been doing some work there."

Sam already had a team? Joy swallowed her surprise.

His commitment to this project was amazing and inspiring.

"I saw all the lovely decorations going up in the square when I was out walking earlier." Miss Partridge frowned. "But my dear, I'm not an actress."

"We don't want an actress to speak for Sunshine. We want someone genuinely interested in this town. Someone who will promote all it has to offer from their heart. Someone who really cares. That's you," Sam assured her. "In all the years I've lived at the ranch, you've been the best spokeswoman this town has ever had."

"Me?" Grace glanced from him to Joy, who felt compelled to nod her agreement.

"Please, give it a try," Sam begged. "Come with us to the square and we'll do a little run-through. I'll record you on my phone so you can see what I have in mind."

Speechless for probably the first time in her entire life, Miss Partridge stood staring at them until Sam reminded her that Joy needed to get home to feed her children.

"Yes, I do, because my sitter today is Sam's sister-in-law and she has her own family to care for," Joy agreed. "But I have a bit of time yet. Try it, Grace. Give Sam a chance."

After a moment of shocked silence, Miss Partridge fetched her purple beret and coordinating scarf and gloves without uttering another word. Sam held her beautiful black suede coat as she slipped into it, praising her wardrobe choice.

"You look fabulous," he said as he opened the front door.

"Thank you, dear. I'll drive myself over and meet you there. That way you won't have to drive me back, and Joy can get home more quickly. Oh, my. A commercial.

Who would have…?" Miss Partridge closed the door behind them.

"Isn't she coming?" Sam said, looking confused.

"She goes out the back way to the garage." Joy was amused to see that the two most confident people she knew appear so utterly discombobulated. "You're sure about this?" she asked as Sam drove to the square. "I don't want Grace to be hurt if she's no good."

"Just wait," Sam told her confidently.

Grace Partridge scanned the script he showed her, pursed her lips and nodded.

"I can't do verbatim tonight, but I get the drift of what you want. I'm ready to try it," she said, taking the position Sam indicated.

Joy blinked in surprise when a big white metal sleigh with gigantic red bows on either slid to a stop next to the sidewalk, as if waiting for its next passengers. The sleigh was harnessed to six matched stallions that Joy knew came from Hanging Hearts Ranch. Drew and Mandy sat in the front of the sleigh, wearing white Stetsons and red scarves. Their kids sat behind them, snuggled under a red furry robe with white trim, their wide grins proof they were having the time of their lives. Somewhere in the background the faint chimes of a Christmas carol played.

"Okay, go," Sam called.

"Hello there. I'm Grace Partridge."

Sam was right. The woman was a natural. Joy couldn't help admiring her poise and confidence while reciting a script she'd barely studied, all the while being recorded.

"Welcome to my hometown of Sunshine. We're getting ready to Experience Christmas. That's our local Advent Festival. It offers something fun and exciting is happening here in Sunshine every day, until the celebrations culminate in our Christmas Eve potluck. If you're not experiencing Christmas the way you'd like, why not join us?" She paused, blinked.

Joy turned her head to see what had caught Grace's attention. Two deer stood under the glow of a streetlamp at the edge of the woods. She noticed Sam was now filming the pair.

Grace's whispered voice cut in.

"Seems like you-know-who sent some friends to check out our festival," she murmured for the camera. Then as the deer bounded away, she chuckled merrily. "They'll sure have a lot to tell that jolly man. So why don't you join us? Trust me, you've never experienced Christmas our way. Hope we see you soon." She waggled her gloved fingers, stepped forward to accept Drew's helping hand into the sleigh and then sank down gracefully onto the seat between the children. Suddenly she leaned forward.

"I almost forgot! For more information please check out our website, ExperienceChristmas.com." She waved one hand toward the horses. "On, Dasher, on, Dancer," she called with a merry laugh.

The sleigh pulled away as, one by one, Christmas trees along the roadside lit up like a path to follow.

"Cut!" Sam called. He walked over to Joy. "Well? What do you think?"

"I think she's perfect." It came out as a whisper because Joy could barely find her voice. "I think you're amazing." Then, embarrassed by her effusive tone, she added, "I think I need to get home."

Sam laughed wholeheartedly, every handsome feature of his face highlighted by that amazing smile.

"Drew's coming back now, Joy. As soon as Miss Partridge is on her way home, we'll leave," he promised.

Joy stood beside him, savoring the sound of the horses' clopping hooves. And then it started, that faint first ripple of anticipation at the prospect of Christmas. She hadn't felt that in years. It was exactly the feeling she wanted her children to have. In fact, it was an intricate part of the perfect family Christmas she so desperately wanted Josh, Becca and Cris to finally experience this year.

"Dad made that sleigh years ago when a really long, cold winter kept him inside in the evenings," Sam explained. "We always go for a ride at the ranch on Christmas night as a family. But I thought it might be fun to offer rides through the forest outside of town and back as part of Experience Christmas."

"What a great idea. And what a creative man Ben is." Joy smothered her laughter as Miss Partridge descended from the sleigh like a princess.

"Sam?" the lady demanded, marching to where they waited. "Tell me I didn't just lie. Do we even *have* a website?"

Joy winced at the word *lie*, wondering if Sam was offended by it.

"Being built as we speak." Apparently, he wasn't bothered because his smile never diminished as he touched Grace's shoulder to show her what he'd recorded. "You did an awesome job, Miss Partridge. But then, I knew you would. Can we shoot a couple of other short segments tomorrow? I want to have a variety to run."

"Sure, if you text me the scripts tonight so I can study them," she agreed, but she wore a frown. "Won't advertising be terribly expensive?'

"It would indeed. But we're not going to pay for our advertising," Sam explained. He paused to thank Drew and Mandy before turning back to Grace.

"We're not?" Grace glanced at Joy, who shrugged because she had no explanation.

"Nope. We're going to put them on YouTube. We'll

feature different ones on our website and we'll send out tweets, too. Plus we're going to put up posters and hand out pamphlets."

"YouTube," Miss Partridge whispered, her blue eyes wide with something Joy couldn't define. "Maybe they'll go viral. Maybe through this the Lord will lead me to that special man I've been searching for..."

Joy blinked her surprise that this straight-laced woman was looking for love. Here was proof that everyone had deeply hidden desires.

"You're looking for romance?" she asked.

"Now that I've retired from the library, I'm ready for new horizons. Who knows if God has romance in store for me?" Miss Partridge smiled. "Can I see what you videoed again, Sam?"

"Yes, but tomorrow, after I tinker with it. We may re-shoot and there are a few things I want to move around, too," he told her then winked. "Not much though, because you were fantastic."

"Well, I changed your script a lot," Grace murmured. "I couldn't remember exactly what you'd written so I ad-libbed."

"So what?" Joy shrugged. "I thought it was perfect, especially when the deer showed up."

"That was particularly special." Miss P. glanced up into the night sky. "Our Father sent a little surprise. Confirmation that He has His eyes on us." She patted Joy's shoulder. "Now dears, you get on home. Tomorrow's your moving-in day, isn't it, Joy? I'll be there to help however you need me. And Sam, I'll be at the meeting tonight, too. I'm getting really excited about our Experience Christmas schedule."

"Tonight? I thought there was a meeting tomorrow night." Joy blinked her surprise.

"There's one tomorrow night, also," Grace said with a grin. "And probably every night until we really *experience Christmas.*" She waved a hand. "Goodbye, dears."

Joy didn't know what to say as Sam drove them back to the ranch. It was clear this reporter was far more gifted than she'd even imagined. And that he saw untapped talent in the most unexpected places.

"You're doing the website yourself?" How could he possibly keep up with all the jobs that needed to be done in order to pull off this event? she wondered.

"Not me." He sounded relieved. "The teacher from the high school computer lab is helping his students assemble it as a class project. They've got some pretty innovative ideas and they're far more knowledgeable than I am about how to get the word out. I've only been involved in traditional media."

"I don't think you're that much out of step with the world, Sam," she said.

"Glad you think so." He chuckled when she blushed. "Seems I won't be doing any more filming either. Trent Brown just texted me. He was driving home from college and saw us in the park. Once he knew what we were doing, he offered his high-tech video equipment. He'll splice everything together, too. He'll do an amazing job because he's going to use it as his end-of-term presentation."

"You're getting the whole town involved." Why was she surprised?

"That's the idea. This can't be only my promotion, Joy. Sunshine has to embrace Experience Christmas as their own to make it work," he said quietly. "And so far, most of them seem willing to do just that."

Joy thought of his naysayers from that first town meeting and wondered if they would cause problems down the road. But she didn't want to voice her concerns. To-night's filming with Grace had gone amazingly well. Why spoil it?

"Moving day tomorrow," he reminded.

"Yes. I can hardly wait." She hugged herself in hap-piness. "God has blessed me so much, and in sending you to help us."

"I'm not sure God cares much that I'm here." The way Sam said that bothered her.

"That's not right." Joy frowned. "'Casting all your care upon Him; for He careth for you,'" she recited. "That was one of the first verses Miss Partridge had me memorize. Why would you think God doesn't care about you?"

"Experience," he muttered half under his breath as he pulled up in front of the log house.

"He wasn't with you in all your travels?" she asked in a very quiet voice. "Or when you were orphaned before the Halstons took you into their home?"

"Well, maybe then but—I don't know the answers to those questions anymore, Joy." Sam raked a hand through his hair as if he was annoyed. "I used to think God was with me. Until recently. But then…"

Something inside Joy knew he was referring to filing that false report. Again she wondered what had happened. What made him doubt God was with him?

"It doesn't matter," he said, summoning a smile as he braked in front of the log house.

"Of course it does," she informed him sternly. "You can't doubt that God is with us all the time, whether we feel Him or not! That's a big part of having faith."

Sam said nothing, but he didn't look convinced as he got out of his car and went around to open her door. Joy laid her hand on his arm to draw his attention.

"The Bible tells us that God cares about us more than

He cares about even the birds whom He knows intimately. And it says we're worth far more to him than those birds. *You* are worth more. We're His children. Can't you have faith in your Father?" She'd barely finished speaking when the report of something exploding echoed through the ranch. "Was that a car backfiring—Sam?"

He stood frozen and unresponsive, his glazed eyes peering blankly into the distance, his body rigid.

"Sam?" Joy repeated, afraid to touch him, to rouse him out of this—stupor? "Are you okay?" she whispered.

Sam didn't answer her for a long, long time. Her worries grew as she scoured the yard for someone, anyone who could help them. No one appeared. Her fingers had just closed around her cell phone when Sam suddenly roused back to awareness.

"Are you all right?" Joy studied his face, looking for some explanation for his odd reaction. Could it have something to do with his time in the Middle East?

"I'm fine." He managed to smile, but his face was bleak, strained. "Want to check out your van?"

"Not now," she said firmly after glancing at where it sat in front of the little log house. "I'll do it tomorrow. Do you want to come in for supper? The kids—"

"Thank you, Joy, but I haven't spent much time with my parents," he cut in, his words almost inaudible. "I better get home. Good night."

"Good night." But she stood watching as he drove his car to the main house, parked it and then walked inside.

What was wrong with Sam?

Chapter Six

"You're sure you want to take *all* of this stuff?" Sam's eyes widened at the number of boxes piled inside the door of the log cabin. "You do remember that the bakery comes *with* the equipment?"

"I know. But I'm familiar with the way my own pans bake. I'm used to *my* stuff." Thankfully, Joy saw no sign of his odd reaction last night. This Friday afternoon move should go off without a hitch. She smiled and patted his cheek with her mittened hand. "Humor me, okay, Sam? If I end up having to take it all back home, I won't ask you. I'll do it myself."

"Not what I meant," he told her in a droll tone.

"I know." She chuckled when Sam made a face before motioning to his brothers. After Drew and Zac blinked in surprise at all the supplies she, Grace and Clara had organized, the three men began carrying everything out of the log house and into the huge ranch trailer parked in front.

Sam was such a good friend. What would she do without him?

When Joy turned back, she noticed Josh, Becca and even Cris each struggling to carry something to the truck. A smile curved her lips at their sweet efforts to help.

Sam's influence, no doubt. He seemed to have a positive effect on her kids.

"You guys are so great," she said, trying to hug each one, though Josh managed to wiggle free. "How much are you going to charge me for your help?"

"Nothin'," Cris said, huffing as he pushed a box up the ramp toward Sam. "Families help each other. Sam said so."

"Yup, he did." Becca's bag got stuck partway up the ramp. She burst into giggles as Zac swept her and the bag into his arms and carried them both inside the truck. A moment later she scampered out, squealing with delight as he chased her.

"You sure can pay me, Mom," Josh muttered as he flung a sack of towels and cloths up into Drew's outstretched hands.

"What do you want money for?" Joy kept her face impassive as she waited for her son's response.

"Gifts." He didn't look at her. "It's gonna be Christmas soon."

"I heard, son." As Josh swept past her and returned to the house, Joy wondered if she could somehow wrangle enough money out of her squeaky-tight budget to buy him a really special Christmas gift, something other boys his age had and enjoyed. Maybe a video game?

Josh was such a great big brother, taking on responsibility far above his years. He seldom asked for anything. None of her kids did. That was why Joy wanted to make this Christmas an extra-special one. A family one. If only *her* family...

"What's with the frown?" Sam murmured from behind her. "I thought moving day would make you happy."

"It does. Very happy. Just—thinking." She turned and forced a smile.

"Must have been dark thoughts." Sam clapped his gloved hands together as if to warm them. "We're loaded, I think. Want to check if we've left anything behind?"

"Sure." Joy hurried inside the house, but one quick look around told her there was nothing more to take.

"Okay?" Sam asked from the doorway.

"Perfect. Let's get to the bakery." She followed him outside, closed the door then tromped down the snow-covered stairs. "I wish it would have waited to snow until we were unloaded."

"These few flakes won't be a problem when we back up to the loading door," he promised. "Anyway, everything's covered inside the trailer. Can I ask you something?"

"I guess." Now what?

"What does Cris want for Christmas? He says you won't get it for him." Sam lifted one eyebrow in a question.

"No, I certainly won't tell you." Joy scooted past him and into her new van before he could see her burning cheeks. As if she was about to explain to Sam that her youngest son wanted a daddy who would take him to all the father-son events in his Boy Scouts troop!

Joy followed the truck into town, loving the feel of her new van. This vehicle had plenty of room for her kids, and more in the back. Sam had suggested installing some shelves to transport baked goods in the cargo area. It was a good idea. But it would have to wait until the bakery was open and running.

Clara and Grace had finished the Friday deliveries and were waiting at the bakery. With so many helpers and Clara as director, it took very little time to unload both Joy's van and the trailer. Thanks to her assistant's quick help and solid knowledge of how a bakery functioned, everything was in place in very short order.

"We ordered pizza," Sam told Joy once they'd finished. "We can use that big finished room downstairs with chairs and tables to eat in."

"What about up here? At these tables and chairs, where my coffee nook will be?" Joy paused a moment to relish a mental image of the space filled with people sipping coffee and enjoying her baking.

"I thought it might be better if we kept your storefront clean and tidy. Less work today if there are no spills to clean up," Sam suggested.

"Okay, sure." She shrugged.

"Besides, I have an ulterior motive." He grinned that playful smirk of his. "I'm thinking your lower space would work for some of the events we're planning, in addition to the hall. Actually, in place of the hall for the next few days. The work there won't be finished until next Tuesday, I'm told."

"What are the activities?" she asked hesitantly.

"First, a coloring contest for the smaller kids." He expanded on that idea. "We'll have a sitter if parents want to leave their children to visit the booths. It should last two hours, tops. We want the coloring done on-site to make sure the kids do it all themselves. The contest must be fair so they all have an equal chance to win a prize."

"And the second activity?" Joy listened while the baking list for tomorrow filled her head.

"That's going to depend on you and Clara." Sam smiled at her surprised expression. "I'd like to hold the gingerbread contest here. Maybe downstairs?"

"Okay. And—oh." The fuzzy picture in her brain cleared. "You need us to bake the gingerbread."

"Yes." Sam let his hand rest on her shoulder for a minute. "I know it's a lot to ask, Joy," he said seriously. "If you can't do it, we'll figure out something else. You've

already got a ton on your plate with opening this place."
He narrowed his gaze and came up with different scenarios. "We could use cardboard or something in place
of gingerbread. Or have a craft time."

"Cardboard? In place of real gingerbread? I don't think
so," she said with a shake of her head. "We *are* a bakery."
She glanced at Clara. "We can do it, right?"

"If it's later in the afternoon, yes. We'll need to get the
main baking finished first," the other woman explained.
"Then the oven will be free and we can bake large slabs
of gingerbread. They'll need time to cool before your
participants cut them to their specifications."

"Have I told you how glad I am that you're on board?"
Joy said as she hugged her helper. "I'm already shaking.
I'd never manage this all on my own."

"Hey, I'm glad to be back at work," Clara said, returning the hug. "Together we're going to knock off Sunshine's socks."

Joy gave a thumbs-up. Just then a truck horn tooted
at the back.

"That's our frozen order, I hope." Clara motioned
for Joy to stay where she was. "I'll get our product un-
packed and arranged in the freezer the way I like. Then
I'll start panning out for tomorrow. Once that's safely in
the proofer, I'll head home, have a nap and come back at
midnight to start my shift."

"But we're going to have pizza," Grace countered.

"Thanks, but my daughter's making dinner tonight,"
Clara explained with a smile. "I have to be there because this is the first time she's done it. Thanks anyway,
though." She hurried away.

"Panning out? What's that?" Miss Partridge asked.

"It means taking out the frozen pieces of dough we'll
be using and doing whatever we need to prepare them for

baking," Joy explained. "Then they go into the proofer overnight. It's like a moist, warm cubicle that promotes even rising. They'll be ready to bake early the next morning while our other scratch products are rising."

"Sounds very, uh, organized." Sam's disappointed expression made her giggle.

"It is. Not what you we were imagining, dear?" Grace made a face at him.

"I was thinking more about jolly bakers with red cheeks and high white hats hand-preparing everything from scratch and then passing it out as samples," Sam mourned.

"How stereotypical." Joy laughed as she shook her head. "I don't have enough staff or oven space to do that yet. So for now we'll supplement our scratch baking with frozen. But we'll add our secret touches so it will be like no one else's. You'll see," she promised with a wink.

With Clara's departure, Sam's brothers arrived bearing the pizza and two big bottles of soda. Joy's children had disappeared downstairs earlier, so it took only moments before everyone else followed. They were soon seated around the table. Drew said grace before they dug into the steaming pies.

"The first meal in your new digs." Sam tilted back in his chair and glanced around.

"This space has a lot of—um, possibilities. Doesn't it, Sam?" Miss Partridge's eyes twinkled as she studied him.

Joy laughed.

"What's so funny about that?" Sam demanded, looking from one to the other.

"That's who made my bakery possible, remember? That company called Possibilities. I wish I knew how to thank them." Though slightly confused when the Calhoun brothers exchanged a glance that no one seemed inclined to explain, Joy shrugged it off. "My mind is bubbling with ideas for this place. It will be interesting to see how they mesh with your festival events, Sam."

"It sure will." He finished his drink, accepted the children's thanks for the pizza and then began clearing up the mess.

"Oh, I forgot you have that meeting tonight." Grace moved quickly. Before Joy could pitch in, the brothers were wiping the empty tables with damp paper towels.

"Aren't you going, too, Grace?" Surprised when her friend shook her head, Joy let her gaze rest on each one of these special people. "Thank you so much for your help. Please let me pay for the pizza."

"Consider it our welcome to your new business, Joy." Zac grinned. "Know that you can count on our support."

"A lot of support," Drew agreed, licking his lips. "I myself am waiting for your first batch of doughnuts."

"I'll save you the first dozen," she promised.

"Or two," Sam shot back with a smirk.

Within minutes the three men had brushed off her thanks and hurried away to dump hundred-pound bags of flour into two rolling bins and the sugar into a matching container. Then Drew and Zac left.

"The bins are a really good idea," Sam mused. "I wonder if Dad could use something like them for feed, so he's not always lifting heavy sacks."

"There's an old one out back that's dented. Also, one wheel doesn't work," Joy told him. "If you think the dents could be pounded out and the wheel repaired, you're welcome to it. We have enough here."

"Thanks." He dragged on his jacket before pausing. "You okay to lock up and get home?"

"In my almost new van?" She preened for a moment. "More than okay."

"Then I'm off to my meeting." He thanked the kids for their help and told them they'd done a good job.

"Let me know what you need me to do, Sam," Grace reminded him.

"Sure will." Then he was gone.

Funny how the bakery suddenly seemed so quiet, so empty.

"It was nice of them to buy us pizza, wasn't it, Mom?" Josh asked.

"Extremely nice." She hugged the kids. "You guys are amazing helpers. And you, too, Grace." She smiled at their proud faces. "Now, I have a couple of things to do before we can go home. You can help me or you can do homework or read."

They all voted to help. After rearranging the tables and chairs in front of the massive covered windows, ready for folks to sit and enjoy a treat and a drink tomorrow, four sets of curious eyes rested on her.

"Now what, Mommy?" Becca wondered when every table sparkled and the old but sturdy chairs gleamed.

"This is a bakery. I need to try the ovens so we don't get a surprise tomorrow. Let's bake." Thanks to the giant floor mixer and Grace's able assistance, Joy soon had a huge batch of shortbread cookie dough mixed up. All three children donned aprons and plastic gloves before they began cutting out stars, Christmas trees, bells and bows.

"We'll need decorations," Grace reminded her.

"Right here." Joy opened a many-lidded tray. "Put some in a small bowl so you don't get the whole batch messy, kids."

The kids laughed, worked and generally had a ball as they took great care with their cookies. When a baking sheet was filled, Joy slid it onto one of the revolving shelves in the big oven, relieved that according to the thermometer, the oven held its temperature perfectly.

"What a blessing this place is, God," she murmured as she closed the door. "Thank you for providing it."

"It is a blessing," Grace agreed from behind her. "And you are a blessing to Sunshine, too. You and Sam."

At the mention of his name, Joy's cheeks grew warm. She turned away to fiddle with some cooling cookies, hoping to hide her discomfiture.

"You like him a lot, don't you?" Grace sighed as she perched on a nearby stool. "I so envy that."

"You envy me? Why?" The despondency in the other woman's eyes saddened Joy. She wished she knew how to help her friend.

"You probably think it's silly, but I've always wanted to find someone special, a man who'd make my heart quake. Someone who would fill the void in my life." The older woman half smiled. "Everyone thinks I'm just a dowdy librarian who's read too many romance novels. But I so long to share what's left of my life with someone."

"Are you thinking of someone local—" Joy stopped midsentence when Grace shook her head once, firmly.

"Over the years I've considered most of them," she admitted. "And since they've come back to the ranch, Drew and Zac and their wives have tried to help me find someone, too." Her sigh came from deep within. "But God just hasn't seen fit to send me anyone. I guess I'll have to face the fact that I may never fall in love."

After that it seemed to Joy that Grace lost her zest for baking shortbread. They worked together for a little while, but eventually her friend looked so weary that she urged her to go home and rest.

"I'm sure Sam will be hunting you down for some-thing tomorrow," she said, wishing she knew a man who would suit this lovely woman. "I'll pray God sends you a real prince," she whispered as she let Miss Partridge out the front door.

"A prince would be nice, but so would an ordinary man who fell in love with me." Miss Partridge hugged her. "Thank you, dear. You're very kind. Good night." She waved to the kids and then disappeared into the darkness.

Caught up in baking with her kids, Joy pushed away thoughts of Miss Partridge's predicament until later. But she wasn't as successful at dislodging thoughts of Sam and that reminded her of his many comments about the building's newest upgrades. A new outlet installed, a special exhaust fan placed on the ceiling over the fryer that would take care of any fumes from frying doughnuts. He'd shown her the bakery's rejuvenated dishwasher and its modified operational system, too, something Clara said wasn't here during her previous employment.

Now Joy wondered how it was that Sam knew all these things about a place he said he hadn't seen for years. Things like the roof's newly installed gutter system that even the hardware store owner, Marty, hadn't told her about.

"Must be a man thing." A buzzing timer forced Joy to shrug off her questions as she rescued the browning shortbread.

Tonight was for enjoying God's gift of time with her kids. Hopefully, tomorrow the bakery would be so busy, she wouldn't have time to think about anything but filling customer orders.

As if she could stop thinking about Sam.

"Joy's son Josh has been asking me about your bowls, Dad. The ones you left on display in the log house." Sam sat in his car with his phone on Speaker, waiting for his committee members to arrive for their meeting.

He smiled, visualizing his dad's shoulders pressed back with pride. Woodworking was Ben's passion.

"Oh? What's he want to know?" his father asked.

"It seems like he already knows a lot, though I think it's mostly book knowledge," Sam replied. "He asked if he could watch you sometime."

"You bring Josh along anytime, Sam," Ben said eagerly. "I'd like to teach that young man my favorite hobby. I'd like to get to know Joy a little better, too."

"Yeah, we'll have to get everyone together soon." Sam wasn't going to commit to anything that had to do with Joy.

"She's special, isn't she, Sam?" Probing questions were his father's specialty.

"Joy? Yes, she is. Very." How could he steer his dad away from this path? "But I told you. I'm not looking to get involved romantically."

"Because of Celia," Ben stated.

"Partially. But mostly because this just isn't a good time," he said. "There are too many unresolved issues for me at the moment."

"You're hedging, Sam. I've noticed you do that during our little Bible studies, too. You say you want to build a closer relationship with God, but it's like you can't quite commit." Worry edged the sober words. "Why don't you tell me what's going on?"

"I can't, Dad. I can't talk about it. Not yet. I just have to—wait, I guess." *So not your strong suit, Mr. Smart Alec Reporter.*

"What are you waiting for?" his dad pressed.

"The end of what I started in the Middle East," Sam mumbled.

"Any idea of the timeline on that?" Ben responded.

"None. That is what's so frustrating. But I appreciate

your counsel, Dad. And that you don't keep pushing me for answers I can't give." His father had always been a patient man. Sam wished he'd learned more of it.

"There's a verse in Isaiah that fits this occasion. 'They that wait upon the Lord shall renew their strength,'" Ben began.

"Yes, I remember. 'They shall mount up with wings as eagles,'" Sam replied. "'They shall run, and not be weary; and they shall walk and not faint.' Guess I need to keep running, right, Dad?"

"Yes, but more importantly, it seems to me you need to keep waiting on the Lord, as you've been doing," Ben encouraged. "Keep trusting Him to work things out. Even though you may not have heard or seen any results, that doesn't mean nothing's happening over there. God has ways and means of getting things done that that we can't even begin to imagine. Our part is to let Him do it."

"Thanks, Dad. It's been so great to have you counsel me on faith. I got a little adrift when I was over there—lost my bearings, you could say." Sam winced at the truth of that.

"And you've found them now?" his dad asked.

"Not completely. But with your guidance, I think I'm at least getting my feet on the right path." *That sounded weak*, Sam admitted to himself.

"I know you've got that meeting tonight and you're probably ready to head inside for it, but I want to say one more thing."

"Go ahead, Dad. I'm listening." Sam focused on what was to come.

"Don't try to recapture the faith you had, son. I know that sounds odd. But the faith you *had* was for yesterday, last year, different circumstances." Ben cleared his throat.

"I'm still listening," Sam murmured when the silence stretched.

"The faith you're building now will be different. It has to be because you're in different circumstances. You've grown and changed. You want different things." Ben's voice softened. "Don't be afraid when your old faith doesn't seem to fit your life now. It shouldn't. God is changing you, growing your trust in Him."

"But—" He stopped and let his dad continue.

"There will be lots of buts, Sam. Lots of things you'll have to look at with a new perspective. Let Him open your eyes to what could be and forget about what was, including Celia. Let go of what you can't change. He's making you into a new person, His person. God has big plans for the man you're becoming, son." Ben's words died away in the quietness of the car.

In that yawning silence, Sam considered what his dad had said.

"Thank you," he murmured, deeply moved.

"Welcome. Now get into that meeting. Your mother and I will be praying," Ben assured him.

"Your praying has always been the best part of having you both for my parents. Bye, Dad." Sam hung up. He sat for a few minutes, trying to tuck the wise words into the recesses of his mind to think about later. A tap on the window roused him.

Joy. She must have decided to join tonight's update meeting.

His heart grew light and happy at seeing her smiling face.

He'd have to think about that, too.

Chapter Seven

"You want us to hold what?" The entire planning group gaped at Sam.

Joy hid a smile as she glanced around the room, mentally cheering, *Go, Sam.*

"Outdoor movie nights." He chuckled, looking completely at ease amid their disbelief. "In the square. Friday and Saturday nights until Christmas. That backdrop of spruce trees will make a perfect place to put up a sheet or something for a screen."

Joy noticed how many of the festival volunteers struggled to keep straight faces.

"Movies? Outside? In the middle of winter?" the mayor asked in dismay.

"In the cold, dear?" Even Miss Partridge's expression conveyed concern.

"Unless the temperature really drops, yes." Sam grinned. "We'll bring risers from the fairgrounds for seating. We can advertise for folks to bring blankets and—"

"Yes! And if people come without blankets, Maisie Crane can fill a booth with those lovely comforters she makes and sell them," Miss Partridge interjected, her smile wide.

Trust Miss P. to jump on board. Joy appreciated the woman's spirit more with each encounter.

"Another idea. Maisie might also agree to sell some of those fleece blankets the town bought three years ago. They were supposed to be sold for publicity purposes, but never were," the former librarian reminded everyone. "Such a shame. Anyway, we could give them away. Or sell them for cost. Either way Sunshine would get free advertising when our guests take them home."

"Hey, those blankets cost us a lot of money!" Evan Smith bellowed, obviously irritated at the suggestion. Joy wasn't sure why he'd bothered to show up tonight. He'd been no help at all.

"They did cost a lot, Smith, and you're the one who insisted the town buy them. Like those two hundred mugs you insisted council buy when you were mayor. We didn't pay for that stuff to sit on some shelf in the town office, unused!" someone else hollered. "Why don't you pitch in and help here, instead of knocking every idea?"

"Mugs. Oh, my, yes. We'll need those." Miss Partridge clapped her hands together in delight. "For the hot chocolate we'll serve at the movies, of course," she elucidated for those who stared at her. "Joy could have one of her staff circulate with some lovely gingerbread and shortbread cookies for sale, too. Couldn't you, dear?"

"Of course." Joy nodded, delighted by the way Miss Partridge expanded and built on the simplest ideas.

"But—it's ludicrous," Evan sputtered. "It's *winter*!"

"So? These ideas are innovative and fun, totally different from anything this town has ever tried," Marty from the hardware store called cheerfully. "Great concepts. What else have you planned, Sam?"

"I've got a whole list of things we could try. Here are a few." Sam clicked his computer mouse and a colorful presentation illuminated the wall. "The festival will begin Wednesday evening with a simple snowman contest for all age groups. Only we'll provide the articles used to decorate those snowmen. They will *not* be the traditional hat and carrot nose usually seen in pictures."

Laughter bubbled up when he winked. Sam was so great at this. Joy wondered why Evan and his buddies couldn't get on board with the festival.

"We'll follow the snowman contest with a wiener roast, during which our mayor will cut the ribbon and officially declare the opening of Experience Christmas. Then he'll talk about events that will lead up to our Christmas Eve potluck."

"Ooh, I like that idea," someone else in the crowd called. "People of all ages will show up for a ribbon cutting just to hear what's planned. As business owners, we can capitalize on that by running *kickoff* specials."

"Great idea." Sam consulted his list again. "On Thursday, the high school students will show off their ice-carving abilities in the town square. Their art teacher tells me they've been practicing that. Then we'll invite anyone who wants to try it. We could offer a prize—maybe an ice-fishing outfit? At the same time, we'll hold a pizza party contest for younger kids, at the hall because I've been told the work will be finished by then," he added quickly, before someone could ask.

"And Friday?" Miss Partridge's face almost glowed with excitement. "What shall we plan for Friday, dear?"

"We could run several events, all happening on Friday. Most prominent would be a puppet theater to help draw in families. Kids could participate by making their own puppet after the show. You all know Sarabell Edwards is a master crafter at puppet making." Sam grinned at the nods circulating around the room.

"Nobody can top Sarabell," an attendee agreed loudly.

"That will be followed by other events, all geared to family participation. Popcorn-ball making, snowball fights, gingerbread-house decorating." The former reporter smiled as he glanced around the room. "As we see which events are most successful, we'll repeat them throughout following weeks so nobody misses a chance to enjoy any activity."

Joy noticed Sam didn't need to consult the list before him.

"What's next?" Miss Partridge asked.

"Saturday will feature displays of the vendor stalls where they'll show off their crafts and techniques. There will also be hourly retail happenings, opportunities for each business to plan something special for their customers. Saturday nights we'll have consecutive stage performances, which I hope will culminate in a major talent show on the last Saturday before Christmas." Out of breath, Sam leaned back and waited for the group's response.

A rush of pleasure tickled Joy when his glance rested on her. She was so proud of him. This man was proving everything she believed about him. He *was* honorable. It was odd how readily she'd come to believe in Sam, despite a niggling impression that there was something important he hadn't told her.

That first night, when he'd appeared out of the blizzard to rescue her and her kids, and found a safe place for them to stay—that was when her faith in Sam had grown its initial roots. He'd taken responsibility for the tree and made it right—actually, far more than right—by taking them to live in the log house. Nothing he'd said or done since had changed her certainty that this man was honest, true to his word, straightforward and dependable.

It was the same with Experience Christmas. Sam's ideas were amazing. Joy had every confidence he'd see them through each stage of the festival with panache and sure-handed guidance.

Sam was nothing like Nick, who'd often promised great things but faltered whenever the going got tough. It had taken Joy a long time to accept that she couldn't depend on Nick's promises. Since the day she'd understood that, after her parents had rejected her for the second time, Joy had never let herself depend on anyone.

But then Sam appeared in her world and glimmers of believing in someone again had teased her. Since that first stormy night, he'd proven himself over and over.

Though Joy hadn't wanted to leave her kids with Kira this evening, she was glad she'd come. She was more than impressed by Sam and his leadership of the volunteer group's preparation for the festival. But some people weren't.

"Who is going to pay for all this food you're giving away?" Evan wanted to know. "And what are the prizes? Why would anyone come to Sunshine for such ordinary events?"

"The food is budgeted into our figures. And people will come because folks love sharing Christmas. Experience Christmas is designed to bring people together to *share* the joy of Christmas, not least through our fantastic outdoor activities and presentations. We're going to show the world how to celebrate a real family Christmas."

Joy had loved that idea of a family Christmas since she was a lonely only child. She'd yearned for but never enjoyed the jubilant kind of Christmases filled with affectionate relatives that she'd read about in stories, seen on television and watched her friends enjoy. While other kids dreamed of gifts, Joy had been alone, imagining a big gregarious family to celebrate with while her parents relaxed and enjoyed the day off from their busy bakery. But at least she'd had her parents to share the day with— until they'd disowned her.

Nick had been a nonparticipant at Christmas, often disappearing to some place he never talked about. That had made it very difficult to provide the kind of Christmas Joy wanted to give her children. She ached for them to have fun and cheery Christmas memories with an abundance of love and laughter surrounding them. Instead, for the past two Christmases Joy had needed to work at catering parties, desperate to earn the overtime bonuses that would pay her bills. This year she desperately wanted to make the Yuletide something her kids would never forget. Maybe Sam and his family would be a tiny part of the kids' celebrations this year, too?

Joy shook off that wayward thought and the thrill that went with it to pay attention to Sam. He was actually smiling at his detractor. Could he really do all he was claiming?

"As to prizes. Here's the pièce de résistance, Evan." Sam paused. A hush fell in the room. "Every person who purchases an event ticket at our festival will have an opportunity to win our major Christmas prize."

"*Major* prize? Like what? A soda pop?" Evan's surly tone doused the joy in the room. "Wow."

"A free dinner?" asked one attendee hopefully.

"Maybe a winter vacation in Glacier National Park?" guessed another.

Though Sam kept his expression blank as others began calling out possible prize suggestions, Joy could see the gleam in his eyes. She knew he had something special up his sleeve. Finally Miss Partridge asked for silence.

"Well, Sam?" the mayor demanded. "What is this prize?"

"A seven-day vacation package," Sam said clearly. "As well as an appearance on national television with Adelia Forsyth when she covers the Rose Bowl Parade in Pasadena, California, on New Year's Day."

Amid gasps of surprise, Joy saw how proud Sam was of his achievement. His shoulders pushed back and his chin lifted, as if he was daring Evan Smith to denounce that. Meaning he was still friends with some of his colleagues, that they hadn't all turned against him?

"It's an all-expenses-paid excursion, including side trips to several famous parks," Sam added.

No one spoke. Mouths hung open as folks gaped.

"So Adelia's still talking to you after all your lies?" Evan's cunning smile matched the nasty glint in his contemptuous gaze. "I thought your old cohorts had all abandoned you. So why is she doing this? How are you paying her?"

Audible gasps at his temerity filled the room. Appalled, Joy studied Sam, who avoided her gaze. The color drained from his face. His shoulders drooped as he stared at his knotted fingers.

And then—Joy's same nagging worry returned. Something was definitely wrong.

What hadn't Sam told her? What had he omitted? Why had she trusted him?

Sam fought not to show his frustration.

Guilty. Condemned. He'd been tried and convicted, again, without anyone knowing the truth. And now he was handcuffed because he couldn't explain the reasons why he'd given that false story, not yet, not when lives were still at stake.

He'd fought so hard not to cave against the bitterness as the outpouring of anger and frustration swelled against him. In the days since his return to this country, he'd continued the struggle to move past the vitriol, the snide remarks, the whispers of condemnation. To let it slide off his back. To forgive.

Yet every time he turned around, it smacked him in the face again.

This time the denigration hurt more than usual because these were *his* people. This time Sam longed to prove to his hometown that he wasn't the liar he'd been labeled. He loved this place. Sunshine was home, the refuge he'd consoled himself with in the horror-filled days when only God knew where he was.

But truthfully, Sam hadn't striven to come up with fresh, unique ideas for Experience Christmas because he felt guilty about filing that false story. He'd gone to all this work because he truly wanted to share the Christmas joy he'd found in this town, in the foothills of Glacier National Park, when he was an orphaned kid joining a newly formed family. A joy that had resurfaced every Christmas since.

He winced at the knowledge that his bargain to get the Rose Bowl Parade prize would cost him dearly. He'd promised Adelia, his only friend since his other coworkers and friends had abandoned him, that he'd give her a private interview when the time was right. Would baring his soul be for nothing now?

Sam scrambled for a defense to offer Evan but could think of nothing. Apparently neither could Miss Partridge, for she remained silent, glaring at their biggest wet blanket. Joy smiled encouragingly at Sam, though she, too, said nothing. He knew from her expression that she was trying to come up with something, anything that would erase Evan's nasty remark. And she was failing. Because nothing could.

And then, in the tenseness of the silence, a single voice called, "Bravo to Sam."

Thunderous applause followed.

He almost sagged with relief, letting the rest of his team take over the meeting, laying out their plans for each day and asking for support from others where they felt they'd need it. The town's nearly unanimous endorsement of Sam's team's ideas and plans felt awesome. It seemed to him that everyone wanted to be part of Experience Christmas.

Well, everyone except Evan and his cronies who left stomping out of the room.

"All right, people! Now, let me also express the town's gratitude to Miss Grace Partridge. Those commercials she made for our event have gone viral. The town office is getting hundreds of calls every day. Seems everyone wants to meet Sunshine's Christmas lady." The mayor inclined his head at the smiling woman. "You make all of us want to get in the spirit, Miss Partridge."

An appreciative round of applause for the former librarian filled the room.

"Anything else, Sam?"

"I think we've gone over enough for tonight," he said as he rose, satisfied with what they'd accomplished. "If we can get the items on our to-do lists finished, we'll be in good shape by the time we meet again."

Everyone nodded their agreement. Sam, feeling rejuvenated by the support, grinned back.

"Oh, one more thing," he added, and then chuckled at the groans. "If any of you know craftsmen or women in this area who have been hiding their skills or their products, please, please encourage them to participate in our festival. We'll have plenty of booths. There's always room for more artisans because we want to showcase the wonderful skills Sunshine is so proud to have in our town. That's it. Thank you all and good night."

Caught up in a flurry of questions and then making notes for himself on his phone, it took Sam a moment to notice that the room had emptied and he was alone. He switched off the lights and left, figuring that Joy had gone on home, too. Instead he found her standing outside, talking to Miss Partridge.

"Don't be nervous about the hall being finished by next week," Joy murmured in encouragement to the older woman, one hand clasping her shoulder. "They're pushing ahead, working long hours. They've promised it will be ready. We're working on trust, remember?"

"Yes! How good of you to remind me, dear. I have some praying to do." Miss Partridge hugged Joy, fluttered a hand at Sam and called, "Good night, dears," as she hurried toward her bright purple SUV.

"I'd better get home, too. Kira has a test tomorrow." Joy winked. "Good meeting, Sam," she said with a grin. "What a great prize. That must have taken some doing. I'm glad you could pull it off."

This was what Sam really liked about Joy. No questions. Just encouragement and support.

"Thank you. Can I catch a ride back to the Double H with you? Drew borrowed my car to run an errand. I guess I could ask him to pick me up," he added, to give her an out.

"Why bother? I'm going your way." Joy flashed her amazing smile then waved a hand. "The Christmas lights your team have hung all over town are really lovely. Grace just told me an anonymous donor paid to have the town's ancient angel streetlights rewired. They're so pretty."

"Thanks." She gave him a sidelong look as they walked to her van. He pretended not see.

"Grace also said the costumes for the Sunday night play mysteriously arrived after the rental company claimed they wouldn't deliver because they were already booked."

"Yeah, I heard that, too. Nice. Mom calls it Christmas blessings." Sam struggled to hold his nonchalant expression as he tugged open the passenger door of her van.

"Huh. Odd that nobody in this small town knows what changed or who that donor is." She paused to study him. He calmly returned her stare until she finally shrugged. "You have a really great group of volunteers."

When Joy climbed inside the van, the interior lights lent a pinkish tinge to her short, bouncy curls. Once she'd started the motor, she giggled.

"What's so funny?" he asked.

"You seem destined to loan your new car to everyone, Sam, leaving you without wheels."

"That's true." He grinned. "Good thing you have this van."

"Very good thing," she agreed, touching the dash fondly. "A sweet gift from God. Thanks to Him, Mr. Porter and you and your brothers."

They rode in silence for a while. But Sam was beginning to know Joy's silences. This one felt to him as if she was grappling with some internal issue. He opened his mouth to ask about it, then snapped it closed. Best to wait until she told him.

They were moving past her former home when Joy finally spoke.

"Can I ask you something, Sam?"

"Sure." He mentally braced himself.

"Back there, at the meeting. When you announced the grand prize of the festival." She paused, licked her lips.

"Yeah?" They turned in under the creaking sign. Joy pulled up in front of his parents' house, her expression serious. Sam grew more nervous.

"It's just, well, you seemed so—upset," she finally murmured. "Was it because of what Evan said?" She added after a moment of hesitation, "It *was* pretty awful."

He made up his mind in that instant.

"I need to tell you something, Joy." Sam exhaled, desperate to share his horrible burden, to finally have someone on his side. "To explain."

"No." Joy said it quite loudly as she shook her head. "You do not need to explain anything to me, Sam."

"But—" His jaw dropped when she repeated "*No!*" in an explosive fashion.

"Miss Partridge has been trying to teach me to put my trust into action. Okay, then. I will. I trust you, Sam. I trust what you've done for me and my family, and I trust what you're doing for Sunshine and all the families here," Joy said firmly. "I don't need any explanations."

"But I—"

"I trust you, Sam," she repeated very quietly, looking directly into his eyes.

"Thank you." He didn't know what else to say, though inside, his heart was thudding at her kindheartedness.

"You're welcome. Now, I'm sorry, but I need to go. Kira's waiting for me." She smiled as she eased the van into gear but kept her foot on the brake, obviously pausing for him to get out. "Good night."

"I…" Sam let his explanation trail away, realizing that she probably didn't want to hear the whole ugly story anyway. He sure couldn't blame her for that. "Good night, Joy. Thanks for the ride. Sleep well."

Sam got out, closed the door and forced his steps toward his boyhood home without looking back. It had never been clearer than it was tonight: this was a painful, lonely road he had to keep traveling on his own.

But oh, how he'd have loved to have let Joy in on the horrible secret he'd carried ever since he'd illegally crossed that border and begun the most terrifying days of his life, days that lived on still in cold sweats and terrifying dreams. Joy couldn't help him with that.

But You could, God, Sam prayed silently as he entered the house. *You could heal me, release me from all the horror, from reliving it again and again.* He stopped. Then he spoke the question that he usually refused to ask. "Why don't You?"

There was no response.

Trust, he repeated Joy's word. *Trust.*

Chapter Eight

Joy loved this dear old bakery.

Every time she stepped into it, she gave thanks that she had such an awesome place to work.

This morning was no different, but with the festival officially now under way, this first Saturday in their celebration calendar meant she had a ton to do. Beginning with cleaning the snow-covered sidewalk.

Outside it was still dark. Cris, Josh and Becca would be getting up now. Though Joy hated missing their mornings, she'd soon realized that if she made an early start at work, she could spend more time with them later in the day. Thank God for Kira. And Clara.

Yet, Joy was still short a part-time helper in the bakery. She prayed about it as she briskly swept the walk, enjoying the crisp air and the festive lights twinkling around her. How she loved this season of giving. Still, she'd come no closer to figuring out how to give her kids the kind of family Christmas she'd always dreamed of. It didn't have anything to do with things. It had more to do with—

A cold, wet snowball smacked against Joy's cheek. She gave a startled yelp at the chill and brushed away the wetness as she turned to see the thrower.

"Nice to find the old pitching arm still works." Sam stood behind her, flexing one arm, his eyes twinkling with fun.

"Nice for whom?" Joy demanded. Without even thinking about it, she scooped up a handful of snow and tossed it, hitting him squarely on the nose.

"You want a snowball fight at this time of the morning?" he asked, advancing menacingly toward her as he formed another missile.

"No!" Joy shook her head in vehement denial. "Stop it! I have to clean this walk off, not cover it again. Then I need to get to work."

"You win. For now. But I'm only quitting because today is fudge day." Sam dropped the snowball and pointed at the painted words in her display window. "That's going to go over very well with everyone. Especially me."

"Then I really do need to get to work," she said with a grin.

"Yep, which is why I'll finish clearing this snow for you. Provided you save me a big piece of your fudge." He reached out for her broom. Joy gladly handed it over. Her feet felt numb.

"What kind of fudge would you like?" she asked. "I'm making five different flavors."

"Tough decision." Sam began to sweep slowly. "Can I have one of each?" he asked in a hopeful tone.

"Okay, but when you get sick from all the sugar, don't blame me." She grabbed the door handle but hesitated. "How is everything going? Tell me the truth."

"Better than I ever imagined. We're not even one week into the festival and we're getting more visitors than we'd hoped for." He laughed. "Everyone's pitching in to make it a success."

"Because they're led by you," Joy said quietly. "You're their inspiration. We all owe you a debt of gratitude, Sam. Especially me. For the log house, for my van. Even for the bakery, I guess. I know you had something to do with that," she hinted, hoping he'd admit it.

"Nobody owes me anything," he said sternly. "Especially you." Then his tone altered to the familiar teasing. "Now get in there and stir up that fudge, Mrs. Baker."

"Yes, sir." Joy saluted smartly. "See you later?" she couldn't help adding.

"Absolutely," he said absently. She knew his brain was busy working out how to handle the day's activities, especially their first talent show tonight.

Inside, Joy shed her coat in her tiny office, changed her boots to shoes and tied on an apron. Clara was busy slicing the freshly baked specialty breads so there was no use trying to speak to her above the slicer's noise.

Working quickly, Joy assembled ingredients and five flavorings. Within minutes she had her first batch of fudge cooking. Before nine o'clock, all five fudge slabs were cooling and a very large batch of pecan tarts bubbled in the oven. Clara had nearly finished injecting the round doughnuts with jelly.

"Our pastry cases look spectacular," Joy complimented her baker as she admired their work. "We're really full. I just hope we sell it all."

"We will. Especially those little meat pies." Clara sounded certain. "They were a great idea, boss. We can warm them in the microwave so folks can munch on them as they walk around outside."

"Agreed." Joy started a fresh pot of coffee brewing and then unlocked the front door, ready for business even though it was still early. "How did Alyson work out?"

"Our new baker's assistant is a total blessing," Clara

affirmed as she poured herself a cup of coffee. "She's faster than anyone I've ever worked with. Extremely capable. And she loves the hours. Work at night, get the kids off to school and then sleep during the day. She's thrilled with the job."

"Good to hear." Joy tilted her head as the doorbell at the back door rang. "That must be our bread order."

Clara left to handle the delivery. She returned wearing a thoughtful expression. "I think you need to consider finding a different bread supplier, Joy. The quality of this company's product isn't first-class. And we are." She handed over the invoice.

"Yes, we are, Clara. I wish it was possible for us to make it ourselves, but we just don't have the capacity to bake everything. I'd rather bake our specialty stuff because we have a better markup. The grocery store stocks this same bread so there's no competition." Joy tucked the paper into her apron pocket and shrugged. "Still, I'll think about this."

"Think about what?" Sam had walked in on the tail end of their conversation.

"Finding a better bread supplier. My parents made the best bread I've ever tasted. I wish I could get them—" She stopped and shook her head. There was no point in wishing when her parents had made it very clear they wanted nothing to do with her. Ever. "Never mind. We'll just have to manage."

Clara greeted Sam and winked at Joy before leaving to check on the tarts.

"Are you here for your fudge already?" Joy teased.

"Not yet." He beckoned to a group of teens standing outside.

They filed in, shuffling their feet awkwardly, making Joy smile. When they were all inside, he explained.

"They want a really special gift for their drama coach for prepping them for their opening night performance on Sunday night. Since he has allergies, they didn't think flowers were appropriate. I suggested your fudge," he announced proudly.

"Would you like to taste some to help you decide?" she offered. Eager nods had her slicing thin slivers off the solid blocks. She felt a smug whoosh of satisfaction when each teen licked their lips and nodded at one another. They ordered a large box of assorted flavors.

"Are you going to have fudge all the time?" one boy asked.

"I hadn't really thought about it," Joy said. "Why?"

"Because this would be the perfect Christmas gift for my dad, except I don't want to get it too early."

"Why's that, Archie?" Sam asked curiously.

"He scours the house until he finds our gifts," the boy explained with a wry look. "It's hard to surprise him on Christmas. But this would." He finished the last of his peppermint fudge. "It's amazing."

"Tell you what." Joy made up her mind instantly. "I'll make fudge every Saturday. Then you can get your dad's, right before Christmas. Fresh. I could even keep it until you were ready to take it home that evening."

"Okay. Thanks." The boy nodded eagerly.

"I want some of that raspberry fudge for my grandma," another said.

Soon they were all planning gifts.

"Why don't you all put in your orders now? You can buy what you need today and pick up your special gifts on Christmas Eve?" Sam suggested.

When the teens all agreed, Joy quickly wrote up their orders and took their money, thrilled with the sales but a little chagrined by her diminished fudge display.

"Good work, guys. Now, you need to get to practice and I have to go make sure the popcorn wreaths are working out for that preschool class." Sam frowned darkly. "Seems like they always eat most of the popcorn."

Joy burst out laughing.

"It's not funny," he chided and then sighed. "Will you keep a meat pie for me for lunch, Joy?"

"Sure." She set one aside as he and her fudge clients hurried out the door.

"It's like having a blizzard blow in and out in five minutes." Clara reorganized the remaining fudge to make room for more tarts. "That Sam sure has eyes for you."

"Oh, we're just friends," Joy said airily, trying to suppress the thrill that skittered through her at the mention of his name. Thankfully, Miss Partridge arrived then to pick up the rolls for the ladies' auxiliary group who would be selling chili dogs.

"Oh, my dear, the aroma in here." Miss Partridge lifted her patrician nose in the air and inhaled. "Marvelous. Those candy-cane cookies are so darling." She tapped her forefinger against the counter. "Can you give me five dozen? We'll sell them for dessert or with our hot chocolate."

Customers streamed in. Joy kept busy tending to each. She'd intended to be on the sidewalk with samples today, but it was neither possible nor necessary. The bakery swarmed with customers. If they were uncertain, she offered a sample and the sale was made. Their stock was flying out the door. As expected, the meat pies sold out before noon. Happily, Clara had baked two more batches while Joy was selling and they were ready to serve well before lunchtime.

"You're going to have to hire someone to man the counter," head baker Clara said when they finally got a break.

"I know. But—" Joy never got to finish.

"Wages are expensive," the lady interrupted. "But we could probably move more product if there was a second person to help or offer samples outside. And you wouldn't wear yourself out running to clear coffee cups between serving customers."

"You know someone suitable?" Joy gazed at her with new respect. Clara never said anything without a reason.

"Not off the top of my head. But Grace Partridge would know. You should ask her." Clara turned toward the back. "Think I'll whip up another batch of shortcakes. They seem to be popular, and the oven's still hot. We have fresh strawberries and whipped cream we should use up, too."

"But your shift is almost over," Joy protested after a glance at her watch.

"I've got enough time." The lady disappeared just as Grace returned, followed by a mousy-looking woman.

"Hello again," Joy greeted her.

"My dear, we're selling our chili dogs so fast that we need more of your delicious rolls. Are there any left?" Miss Partridge asked.

"Of course. We baked extra just in case. Right here." She pulled the rolling cart forward.

"Oh, where are my manners? Joy, this is Honey Gray. I asked her to come along because I thought you might need an extra pair of hands today. Honey's helping hands are the best," Miss Partridge said cheerfully. "And can she ever sell."

"Hello, Honey." Joy shook the woman's hand. "How kind of you, Grace, and of you, Honey, to offer. Actually, I could use your help now, if you're willing, Honey?"

The woman nodded though she said nothing. After they'd loaded Grace's car with fresh rolls, Joy showed her newest employee how to pack the assorted products for sale so they wouldn't flatten, and how to operate the cash register. At first she had doubts about Honey's capabilities, but there was no time to worry when a crash sounded in the kitchen. Joy left Honey with a client and went to investigate.

"My fault. Just plain clumsiness," Clara grumped as she restacked her baking pans on the stainless-steel table. "Nothing serious."

"I'm glad." Reassured, Joy returned to the front and found it teeming with clients and Honey deftly dealing with each, smiling calmly as she filled orders and rang up sales. It was a simple thing to step in beside her and work together in tandem so no one had a long wait. Joy was thrilled to note that Honey had somehow found time to run fresh coffee.

"We need more meat pies," her helper whispered between customers. Once Joy had retrieved another tray from the back, Honey requested a packaging refill of the pristine white boxes and bags labeled *Joy's Treats*. On and on they worked until nearly two thirty, when a sudden lull offered some breathing space.

"You are a treasure, Honey, and if you want it, you have a job here. Ten to three thirty Tuesday to Friday. Saturday ten till closing," Joy offered on the spur of the moment.

Though an inner voice chirped a reminder about past, quick decisions she'd regretted, Joy shut them down. Honey was the answer to a prayer she'd barely voiced. God was meeting her needs. Joy would trust He would continue to do so.

"I accept the job," Honey said, the faint traces of a smile on her lips. "Thank you, Joy. This is a happy place to work. I like it a lot."

"Great! If you think you can man the store for a bit on your own, I'd like to go out and look around, see how our festival is doing." Joy showed her new helper how to reach her cell phone via the bakery phone's speed dial if she needed help.

Then she tugged on her jacket and gloves and strolled down the street, loving the cheery atmosphere that abounded amid soft Christmas carols filling the air.

A group of kids were engaged in a skating tug-of-war on the pond. Many couples perused the stalls in the park, which were filled to bursting with offerings, providing enough choices for any shopper. Other folks wandered in and out of the stores, arms laden with prettily wrapped packages, a service one of the local clubs offered. An igloo-building contest was in progress on an empty lot. In the distance she saw Drew and his father, Ben, seated on the old sleigh they'd used in the video. Several families sat behind them, their children shaking bells that echoed through the winter air.

People laughed and greeted each other with happy smiles as they moved from venue to venue, store to store, activity to activity. Joy soaked it all in, glad her own kids could be here, somewhere, with Sam's sister-in-law, no doubt having as much fun as anyone. She'd get to hear all about it later.

A car backfired just as Joy's gaze lit on Sam, who stood in front of a ring of trees that marked the outside edge of the park. Her heart gave a bound of delight, until she saw Evan Smith standing nearby. She could tell from the man's raised voice that this was not a happy meeting.

But something else was wrong. Sam's face was white and still, as if he'd swallowed his anger for too long. No, more as if he'd been struck. She quickened her pace, hurrying toward him.

"If a kid is seriously injured on that ice," Mr. Smith snarled, "it will be all your fault and this town will be sued for everything it owns. Nice work, Sam."

Sam seemed frozen in place. He offered no response in his own defense, didn't even look at the other man. Joy's anger burst out of her.

"Stop this!" she hissed. "You're making a scene and ruining everything we worked for. No one is going to get sued, Mr. Smith." Joy had no idea what made her intervene, only that she couldn't let Evan continue to browbeat Sam. She glared at his accuser. "You know very well that this is a shallow pond. The ice is perfectly safe since it's so cold today. Everything is going very well. People are actually enjoying themselves. Sam's done a magnificent job."

Evan Smith harrumphed.

"Is happiness what you hate, Mr. Smith? Would an accident or a lawsuit make you feel better? Would you be mollified then?" She exhaled and glanced at Sam for backup, only to see that he looked completely disoriented. Something was really wrong.

"Now, look here, lady— Hey, what's wrong with Sam?"

"You are what's wrong. Go away, Mr. Smith," she snapped. "Lock yourself in your office where you can glare at everyone you see. Whatever. Just keep your negativity to yourself, away from here, because the rest of us are trying to make this festival work to keep our town going. So either help us or get out of the way."

The man appeared infuriated by her comments, but Joy didn't care about him. It was Sam, with the shaking hands and glazed, vacant expression, who troubled her.

"If this festival fails, Mr. Smith, and if the required amount of money is not raised," Joy growled, her voice low so no one else would hear, "I will publicly accuse you of undermining all the work that's been done, for the simple selfish reason that you don't want Sam's ideas to succeed. I will then put forward a motion at a town meeting saying that since you and your negative cronies caused the festival's failure, you should repay the outstanding loan on the community hall."

"You can't do that," he sputtered.

"Watch me." She slid her hand onto Sam's arm while she stared down Evan Smith. "Now either get on board or get out of our way. We have no more time to waste on your pettiness."

Mr. Smith, after glowering at her for a moment, scowled at Sam, too. Then he turned his back and stomped away. Joy exhaled.

"Well. That went better than I thought." She grasped Sam's hand and tugged, urging tenderly, "Come with me, Sam. You need to eat your meat pie now. I've kept it warm for you."

Exerting every ounce of energy she could muster, she drew him with her toward the bakery. He walked beside her falteringly, as if he was sleepwalking. Joy didn't know what to think. She only knew that right now she had to get him inside, to someplace private.

At the bakery she directed him to the back, and then sat him in a chair while she drew off his coat and gloves. Sam didn't object, didn't say anything. He just kept staring blankly in front of him.

Aware of the customers they'd passed in front, waiting to buy her baking, Joy spared one second to text Grace Partridge. Help!

Confident her friend would soon appear, she then concentrated on Sam. What was wrong with him? What should she do? Unsure of how to help, she cupped her palms around his face, fretting about the ice-cold chill she felt on his skin.

"Sam?" she whispered, smoothing her fingers over his cheeks. "Come back from wherever you are. It's safe here. Evan is gone. You're safe now. Please, Sam, come back."

When he still didn't respond, Joy leaned forward and rested her forehead against his.

"Please, Sam. You're safe. Come back to me."

The rifle shot repeatedly crackled, deafening him. Sam wanted to cover his ears, to run away, but he knew both were impossible. The ropes on his wrists and around his ankles kept him prisoner. Anyway, even if he could move, they'd just repeat the whole agonizing process all over again.

"Sam?" A soft, soothing voice beckoned him from the nightmare.

He didn't say anything. They'd only use it against him, use it to hurt...

"Please, Sam. You're safe. Come back to me."

Back?

Skin like velvet pressed against his face. Was it another trick? A way to get him to condemn himself, to reveal who— He kept his eyes closed, but seconds passed and curiosity overwhelmed him so he slowly opened them.

"Hi, there. You're safe now, Sam," a charming voice reassured him. It matched the pretty face in front of him.

He blinked away the clouds, trying to comprehend where he was. Ah, the bakery.

"Joy?" he croaked, his throat so dry.

"Yes, it's me. Here, drink this."

Sam felt a cup pressed to his lips. The smell of coffee filled his nostrils. He drank then made a face. "I don't take sugar," he said.

"Today you do. A little more." She held the cup to his lips, forcing him to swallow the too-sweet brew. Finally she took it away and replaced it with a napkin-wrapped pastry. "You missed eating lunch, didn't you?"

"Did I?" When was lunch? Sam frowned at the blank spot in his brain.

"Doesn't matter," Joy said. "Take a bite."

He bit into the pastry. Somehow the savory tang began chasing the fog from his mind. Or was that the sugar hitting his system?

"Another bite," she directed.

"Shouldn't you be working?" he asked when he could speak.

"Miss Partridge is covering. Can't you hear her?" Joy teased as she inclined her head toward the front.

"Oh, I'm sure Joy will be having a grand opening, dear," Sam heard a familiar voice insist. "But perhaps it will be in the New Year, *after* our festival. Now how about some doughnuts? I know how Howard likes those."

"She's quite a saleswoman," he mumbled.

"You remember her?" Joy's scrutiny bothered Sam.

"Of course I remember her," he said firmly. "Grace Partridge isn't an easily forgotten woman. Why would you think I had forgotten?"

"Sam." Joy pulled a five-gallon pail up beside him and sat on it. "You blanked out. Zoned out. Whatever you want to call it," she said quietly. "Why did that happen?"

"I had a flashback." He knew it wouldn't be enough. He'd have to give a fuller explanation. He'd have to tell Joy more. But—

"You had a flashback," she repeated, her voice brimming with disbelief. "That's it? That's your explanation?"

"It's difficult to explain," Sam murmured, struggling to find a way to clarify without saying too much. "When

I was in the Middle East, on my last assignment…" he clarified, to be sure she understood.

"Go on." Her wide-eyed gaze rested on him, waiting for more.

"Okay. So, um…" Her huff of irritation at his delay made him smile. "I have to tell this my way, Joy."

"Sorry," she mumbled. "Go on whenever you're ready."

"It's busy out there. This could wait until later," Sam suggested, then shrugged when she very firmly shook her head. "Okay. One caveat. Everything I tell you is between us. Trust me, it's important."

"All right." She nodded.

"So when I was in the Middle East— Where was I?" He paused to marshal the memories into order. "Oh, yes. Well, I entered a country illegally. I snuck over the border actually, because I needed to verify reports sent to me by someone who claimed that the country's leader was not the irreproachable president the world believed, or that he professed to be. In fact, they said he was torturing citizens who didn't agree with his decisions."

"Dangerous," Joy whispered.

"It was, but I had no other choice than to sneak in. Otherwise the government would know I was there, meaning the president would know. But I also needed to get in secretly because this person insisted they were risking their own life and that of their family to get the truth out. They were trusting me to report on it." He paused and exhaled before continuing. "This person said they could all be jailed or even killed if they were found out. I did not want to be responsible for that."

"Sam." Joy inhaled, her face growing paler than he'd ever seen it.

"This person's reports were horrific enough that I felt

the danger to me to get this story was warranted. I still do," he said soberly.

"That's what you meant when you said you would file that false report again," she murmured and shook her head when he nodded. "Oh, Sam."

"I had to take the risk. I can't tell you all of it, Joy. I can only say that I found enough facts and pictures to verify everything I'd been told, and much more besides. But I was captured before I could tell the story." Even now the shock of that capture sent chills down his spine. Sam clenched his fists again, the black cloud hanging over his brain.

"You were—tortured," she whispered. It was not a question. "Now you have PTSD. That's why you go into that daze sometimes. Something triggers it—a sound, a flash, that car backfiring—" she guessed, her eyes stretching wide. "It took you back there and you relived it all."

"You're very observant." Sam sipped his coffee again and shuddered at the sickly sweetness of it, but he knew the sugar had done its job. Reality was returning. "How did you guess?"

"I should have guessed earlier," she said, frowning. "I was a candy striper in high school. The ward where I worked had soldiers with PTSD." She touched his hand. "But Sam, your capture is in the past. It's over now. You can let it go and get treatment."

"I had treatment. But it's not over." He couldn't say more. Not yet.

"What do you mean?" Joy's confusion was obvious.

"I haven't yet reported my story." He clamped his lips together and checked his watch, shocked to see it was midafternoon. He rose, grabbed his jacket and gloves. "I have to go. There's so much to do for tonight."

"Sam." Joy touched his arm. "Let someone else do it. Take a break."

"Like you do, Mrs. Baker?" He brushed a fingertip against her cheek and smiled. "This festival was my idea, Joy, and I intend to do my utmost to make it work. But thank you for rescuing me. I guess the backfire—"

"Sounded like gunfire. I get it." She walked him to the back door. "If you need a break before the talent show, you can always come back here. No one's using the basement today. It would allow you a bit of peace and quiet."

Sam shivered as, for a moment, the memories swamped him. Then, with a silent prayer for help, he pushed free of the darkness and smiled.

"It's a nice offer. You're a good friend, Joy. Thank you."

He brushed his fingers against her velvety cheek once more, soaked in the vision of her lovely face framed by those gorgeous reddish-gold curls and then left. But as hard as he worked for the rest of the afternoon, Sam could not forget the way Joy had sweetly, tenderly drawn him out of his terrible fugue and back to reality.

In fact, it wasn't until much later that night, after a very successful talent show, when he was driving back to the ranch, that something flickered through Sam's mind. He concentrated on that blank spot in his day and thought he heard Joy's voice, angry, challenging.

Either get on board or get out of our way.

Sam vaguely recalled being harangued by Evan Smith right before his brain had gone skittering back into the past.

Get out of our way, she'd said. So… Joy had been defending *him* to Evan? Again?

Feeling childishly thrilled by her support, Sam drove into the yard. After he'd parked, he studied the log house as, one by one, the interior lights blinked out until only the picture window at the front was illuminated.

Joy moved out of the shadows and sat down in the chair in front of the window. She seemed intently focused on something in her hands, perhaps a Christmas gift for one of her kids? Or maybe she was searching for a bread supplier to replace the unsatisfactory one she had. Sam remembered her once mentioning that her parents had baked the best bread in several counties. It had sounded like their bakery was still operational.

Was there something Sam could do about that? Maybe if they knew Joy now ran a bakery… His mind swirled with ideas.

It wasn't right that Joy and her family still had a gulf between them. She needed her parents. Her kids needed their grandparents in their lives. Surely, with a little help, the rift between them could be mended. Joy had been an amazing friend to Sam. There had to be a way to repay his friend.

Sam's brain offered attractive thoughts of something beyond friendship with Joy, but he ruthlessly shoved them down. His work had caused Celia's death. He could never again risk a woman he cared about by placing her in jeopardy. Especially with his unresolved past. Who knew what his critics might do when he finally released his story. The world was a dangerous place and getting too close to Joy could subject her to the ugly negativity Sam faced every day.

But even that didn't end his desire to stop being on the outside, to stop reporting on others' lives and start enjoying his own, to share real intimacy with someone special, someone who had the same hopes and dreams. *And* shared his problems. Someone who accepted him, faults and all, and helped him become a better person.

Not someone. Joy.

The thing was, Sam debated with himself, maybe Joy

only trusted him *because* of the festival and because he'd helped her with the house and her bakery. If she discovered he was her landlord at the bakery, too—that he'd kept yet another secret—perhaps she'd feel beholden. If she knew the truth about his many properties in Sunshine, even though he was managing the festival for the town's benefit, would her trust in him wane? Sam didn't want to risk that, no matter how much he longed for a special relationship.

So what *could* he do for Joy? First on the list—get to know her kids better. Especially Josh. The boy was at an age where a male figure could make a difference. Cris? That kid had a Christmas wish he wouldn't talk about. Neither would his mom. Maybe if Sam could find out what it was, he could help make it a reality. There had to be something he could do for Becca, too. But what? Maybe his mom would offer some suggestions.

After exiting his car, Sam walked into his parents' house with new resolve to help Joy and her kids have the best Christmas they'd had in years.

A part of his brain questioned his motives for getting so involved with this family. But that was swiftly replaced by a different mental image of Joy's pretty face, green eyes shining, her lips stretched wide in that sweet smile of hers as she shared with him the joy of seeing her family so happy that she'd have no need to question why he wanted to help.

All Sam needed to do was find something to make this Joy's best Christmas ever.

Chapter Nine

After a very busy Wednesday, Joy wearily returned home to find only two of her children with Kira.

"Sam and Josh are with Sam's dad," Kira explained before Joy could ask.

Sam again. The man was like a whirlwind—here, there and everywhere, always giving. Joy didn't have the energy to hide her grin at the thought of Sam whirling.

"I asked what they're doing, but they said it was a secret. A *Christmas* secret," Kira emphasized.

"I wanna have a Christmas secret, too," Cris complained, glowering at his beloved truck.

"Maybe you will, sweetie," Joy soothed as she brushed a kiss on his brow. "We still have lots of time until Christmas."

"Three weeks, our Sunday-school teacher said." Cris stared at her thoughtfully. "Is that enough time to get my—"

"No, honey. And please don't ask me again," Joy begged, cutting him off. "I've told you. I just can't get what you want. I'm sorry but it's simply not possible."

"God could get it for him." Becca danced her doll across the area rug then tilted her head to peer at her mother. "But Cwis hasta pway lots. Then maybe God'll give him what he wants. Hey, whaddya want?" she added with a sideways glance at her brother.

"It's a secret." Cris glared at her.

"No, it's not 'cause Mommy knows." Becca smiled when Joy knelt beside her. "You don't hafta 'splain to me. I already know, Mommy. You tole me, 'member? You said thewe's lots of secwets at Cwismas."

"There sure are. It's best not to ask about them because you don't want to ruin any surprises." Joy tugged gently on her daughter's ponytail. "I think it's a great idea for Cris to pray about it, though. Good for you for thinking of that. But you both know God doesn't always give us what we want. Sometimes He says no."

And I'm pretty sure He's saying no to your Christmas wish for a daddy to take you to the Boy Scouts' father-son events, she wanted to warn Cris.

"An' sometimes He says yes." Becca always saw both sides of the argument.

"Right. Anyway, now I want you to thank Kira for watching you. She has to get going to town with her friends." Joy smiled at her kids' caregiver, thrilled she had someone so reliable to watch them. Thanks to Sam. Again.

After assuring Joy she'd put the meat loaf in the oven at the requested time, Kira hugged the kids, promised she'd see them tomorrow and then raced out the door. Joy put vegetables on to cook and made a salad while humming along to the carols playing on her phone. She'd just finished setting the table when Josh appeared with Sam.

"Hi, son." Her smile drooped when she saw the dust and shavings covering the front of his coat. "Maybe you need to step outside and shake that off?" she suggested. While he did so, she frowned at Sam. "I thought you'd be in town preparing for tonight's activities. Cross-country skiing by lanterns, wasn't it? I'm sorry if Josh took you away from the festival."

"He didn't. This was something we'd planned to do." Sam shook his head when she raised her eyebrows expectantly. "Don't ask."

"Cwismas secwets. That's what Kiwa tole Mommy. I like Cwismas." Becca raced over to hug Sam's knees. "Are we gonna—"

"Hang posters tomorrow afternoon?" Sam finished. He mussed her hair before turning to face Joy. "I'm not sure. I forgot to ask your mom."

"Yes, you did." Why was she irritated? Joy wondered. Because Sam hadn't asked her to go along? But that was silly. She had several special orders to prepare, as well as more gingerbread to bake for tomorrow's cookie-decorating contest. Miss Partridge had phoned three times to revise the cookie order as registration for the event swelled.

"I'm sorry, Joy. I meant to ask you days ago, but time got away from me." Sam's expression resembled Josh's when she'd caught him with his hand in the cookie jar. "The purpose of the trip is to put up more posters in the next county, as well as speak to a couple of artisans about displaying their work in our festival. One is a very unique potter and the other does amazing fiber art, neither of which our festival has."

"I see." Joy nodded. Sam was going all out for the festival. That wasn't new.

"I hoped the kids could come with me after school tomorrow. Kira could have the time off and I could show them some new countryside. I'd feed them supper, so you won't have to worry about that." As if he had to persuade her further, he reminded, "You usually work a bit later on Thursdays, don't you?"

"Yes." Was that a dig that she wasn't home enough? Joy shoved that thought aside. Sam didn't make digs.

Yet something about his offhand attitude seemed forced. That sent a tickle of worry up her spine, and not because she was concerned about her kids being with him. Sam was great with them. So she tried to home in on what exactly bothered her. Maybe it was his eyes that made her feel he wasn't telling her everything.

"I suppose it's okay." What else could she say with the kids listening in?

"Thank you!" He grinned as if she'd granted his dearest wish. The man sure got excited about putting up a few posters. "If you'll tell Becca and Josh's school and Cris's day care that I'll be picking them up, we'll get on the road right after school." His face altered, his voice turned sympathetic as he laid his hand on her arm. "Don't worry, Joy. I'll be very careful. You can trust me."

There it was again. Trust. As if God was nudging her to remember her goal to accept whatever He sent her way. Yet those bad decisions from her past and the repercussions from them kept hounding her brain, reminding her that she hadn't always exercised the best judgment. Trying to make her feel like a failure.

The doubts will come, Joy. They'll try to beat you down, to tell you you're not good enough, that you aren't capable, that you can't reach your goals. Miss Partridge's words at their shared lunch yesterday returned. *That's when you dig in your heels and refuse to be swayed. In all your ways acknowledge Him and He will direct your paths.*

"The children will enjoy a change. And I hope you're able to persuade these artisans to join our festival." Joy quashed her doubts. "We could use new displays and more vendors."

"Sure could." Sam seemed—relieved?

"If you happen to see any bakeries, get their card, will you? I really need a new supplier for my regular bread order." Joy sighed. "We're getting a lot of complaints about the quality of the stock that's brought in from the city bakery."

"Oh?" Sam stared as if she'd asked him for something very unusual. "Sorry." A moment later he'd recovered his grin as he sniffed the air. "Man, it smells good in here."

"It's just meat loaf." Joy studied his expectant face and gave in to her desire to spend a few more moments with him. "Would you like to share it with us?"

"I shouldn't. I traded the afternoon with Miss Partridge so she could have tonight off. I should be heading for town." But it sounded like he wanted to stay.

"Kira put it in the oven for me earlier so we could eat right away. You do have to eat," she prompted him, hoping, praying he'd stay.

She enjoyed his company a lot. She also wanted to know if he'd had any more of those PTSD episodes.

"You talked me into it," Sam said jokingly. "Thank you."

He quickly shed his coat and boots, took his turn washing up and then sat down at their table. After he'd said grace, he helped each of her children serve themselves while Joy poured their milk.

"No ketchup for me, thanks," he declined when she held up the bottle. "I prefer to taste the meat."

To Joy's great amusement, her sons copied Sam's actions. But Becca had no such inclinations.

"I like ketchup with meat loaf," she insisted as she squeezed a huge dollop on her food.

"Determined. Takes after her mom, I'd say," Sam muttered quietly, snorting with laughter when Joy gave him the stink eye.

It was a great meal, full of fun and speculation about the upcoming weekend events planned for the festival. Though Josh seemed disinclined to talk about his afternoon with Ben, Joy's weariness melted away when Sam related a touching story about a Christmas from his childhood.

"Is the shop hop on Saturday an idea from your youth?" she asked.

"Oh, no. When I was a kid, we never had shop hops in Sunshine. I stole that idea from the quilters in Missoula. They have shop hops once a year. Quilters visit businesses in the area and collect stamps or fabrics. It's different from how ours will be, but the same basic idea." He raised an inquiring eyebrow. "Are you ready for Saturday? We're anticipating big numbers given all the calls we've received."

"Oh, I think we'll have enough taffy for any and all participants who want to pull it," she assured him with a chuckle.

"I might give that a try myself." He pushed back his chair. "I'd better get going."

"I'm sure Grace will have everything under control." Joy's teasing turned into a full-blown smile when Sam rolled his eyes.

"Of course she will. Control is her middle name." He shook his head. "Seriously, she's amazing." He turned to the kids. "So I'll pick up all of you tomorrow afternoon," he reiterated as he shrugged into his coat.

Joy smiled at their enthusiastic nods.

"I enjoyed your cooking very much, Joy," he said, his eyes darkening to unreadable orbs. "Again. Thank you for asking me to share it with you."

"Anytime." When had that tiny fan of worry lines around his lips appeared? she wondered. After the PTSD episode? "I hope you won't have to work too late this evening. Ski time is followed by a snack at the hall, right?"

"Yes. Every time the thermometer dips or the wind kicks up, I ask for a special blessing on those plumbers and electricians who finished work on the hall early. Without them…" Sam shook his head. "'Nuff said." He waved. "Gotta go. Good night. Sleep well."

"You, too." Joy watched him leave.

She turned and saw Josh directing his siblings as they cleared the table. Her heart pinched with love. He was such a responsible son. He deserved a happy, carefree Christmas where he could relax and just be a kid again. A time when he didn't have to feel responsible. A chance to let others take over. If only she could give that to him. If only…

"I like Sam," Cris said. He came to stand by her, his hand threading into hers. "I wish he could be my dad."

"I know you do, sweetheart." Joy bent and hugged him close, stuffing down her own wishes. "I don't think that's going to happen," she said, trying to let him down gently. "But Sam is our very good friend, and tomorrow he's taking you all on a trip. You can enjoy that. Right, son?"

"Yeah. I guess."

It wasn't the wholehearted response Joy wanted from him, but she couldn't do anything about that because her own expectations about Sam needed adjusting, too. He'd done a lot of things to help them. Probably more than she even knew, but nothing that even hinted he wanted more from her than friendship.

For which I should be thankful, she reminded herself when the kids were tucked in bed and she was seated before the fire with her Bible lying in her lap. Atop it lay a list of local bread suppliers, none of whom wanted to drive all the way to Sunshine for deliveries. *Why did I ask him to check out the bakeries? This whole stage in my life is about managing on my own, about not depending on anyone.*

Not depending on anyone? Who was she kidding?

Joy was sitting in the house Sam had found them. She drove the van he and his brothers had helped her acquire. She now ran her business from the old bakery building thanks to Sam's help, and she was far exceeding her sales because of Sam's Experience Christmas plan.

She was very dependent on Sam Calhoun. And she liked that. A lot.

But what would happen when he wasn't there for her anymore?

And that day *would* come. Because it always did.

Joy was a single mother, raising three kids on her own, running a business on her own. If something went wrong, she'd have to face the consequences on her own.

With God, she reminded herself.

She glanced at her Bible. In Him was where her trust belonged.

Best not to forget that.

Sam enjoyed the kids' happy chatter as he drove to the next county. It helped drown out his guilt at not telling Joy the truth.

"We sure are going far," Cris said from the rear seat. "How much longer?"

"Twenty minutes or so. Why don't you read Cris another book, Becca?" He could feel Josh's stare. "You okay?"

"Yeah. Thinking about my project for Mom."

"Dad says the rolling pin you're making for her is

going to be amazing." Sam grinned at the boy. "And a big surprise."

"Maybe." Josh peered out the window. "Are we going to put all those posters up in one town?" It wasn't the first time Sam had noticed the boy's acuity.

"Not sure. Have to see what's already there." Sam turned on the radio, more to cut off Josh's questions than to hear a Christmas carol. But the noise didn't erase a creeping feeling of guilt. He *should* have been honest with Joy about this trip.

Finally they took the exit leading them into the town. They stopped several times. Sam insisted the kids stay in the car while he put up signs. Then he used his GPS to locate the two artisans he wanted to speak to. The kids sat quietly, watching as each demonstrated her craft. They left with the assurance that both craftspeople would be in Sunshine on Saturday, and if that was successful, they would return.

Back in the downtown area, Sam noted the businesses along the main street. Finally he saw what he'd been secretly looking for.

"Can you guys stay in the car for a couple minutes?" he asked. "I'm going inside to ask about the best place to eat."

The younger two both nodded, their interest held by a kid on a sled across the street in the park. But Josh frowned.

"In there?" he asked, inclining his head toward the bakery.

"Yep. I'll be right back. Everyone stays in the car. Josh, you're in charge." Slightly uneasy at leaving them, Sam walked inside the bakery, positioning himself so he could see his car out the window.

He sure hoped this would work out.

"Can I help you?" A small, older woman with a mop of gray curls and emerald-green eyes smiled at him.

"I hope you can. I'm wondering if the owners of this bakery would be interested in supplying *our* local bakery with bread. I'm afraid ours doesn't have the capability to produce regular bread as well as their specialty items." He held his breath before asking, "Would you be the owner?'

"My husband and I are. I'm Greta Coyne. My husband's in the back prepping for tomorrow's bake. I'll ask him." She hurried away.

Sam peered out the window. The kids were still in the car, apparently having fun because they all three were smiling, though Josh was staring at him through the glass.

"Hello. I'm Max Coyne. And you are?" A big, burly man covered in a white apron stared him down.

"Sam Calhoun. From Sunshine. Nice to meet you." He shook the man's hand, awed by the strength in it. "I was just telling your wife—"

"She told me." The man frowned. "I thought Sunshine's bakery had closed."

"It was recently reopened," Sam said. "It's doing well, but there just isn't enough equipment to enable baking all the bread they need. The current supplier's isn't of the quality which the owner wants. I saw your building as we were passing and wondered—"

"Who's the new owner?' Max demanded.

"Her name is Joy Grainger." Sam kept going even though the man's curious expression had turned into an angry glower. "She's a single mom with three kids," he added quickly. "In fact, those are her kids in the car there." He pointed. "We're having a Christmas festival in Sunshine and we came to speak to some artisans—"

"Did Joy send you?" Greta murmured, her eyes on the children.

"No. She doesn't know I'm here." Sam saw longing well in the woman's green eyes. They were a mirror image of Joy's. "I've noticed how disappointed she's been in the regular bread orders. Since she's working so hard to make a go of things in her new business, I wanted to help. I thought perhaps you might—"

"Can't do it," Max said briskly. "We have enough work supplying our own customers. Sorry."

"She's your daughter, isn't she?" Sam paused then added, "And those kids in the car are your grandchildren. They need you in their lives, you know. They have no one."

"Sounds like they have you." Max's brusque response was given through gritted teeth.

"I'm not family." Sam waited, silently praying that this man's heart would soften.

"Joy turned her back on her family years ago. We haven't spoken to her in ages," Max snarled.

"Then isn't it time you did? Isn't it time you got to know your grandchildren, gave them some history? Loved them?" Sam paused only a moment. "They're wonderful children. But they need the backing of family to help them through life. Isn't that what you had when your father started this place?"

"How dare you?" Max's glowering countenance darkened even further, but Sam couldn't give up.

"One day it might be too late and then how will you feel?" he murmured.

"Look, Joy went against our beliefs."

"She made a mistake, Mr. Coyne. We all do. Haven't you?" *Shouldn't have said that*, he thought as the man visibly seethed.

"She hasn't contacted us, even though you say she's so close." Mrs. Coyne couldn't tear her eyes away from his card.

"She contacted you after her husband died and you sent her away—a pregnant mom with three kids to feed." Sam knew he'd hit too hard because Joy's mom was now sobbing.

"Let it go," Mr. Coyne ordered, seemingly unmoved. But Sam couldn't leave things this way.

"Just because you disagreed with Joy, because she followed her heart, doesn't mean she stopped being your daughter," he insisted. "Anyway, she's asked you for nothing since."

"That's true, honey," Joy's mom said.

"Joy's pushed ahead, building a life for herself and her children alone. And you've missed it all. Every one of the kids' birthdays, their achievements, their baby steps, their growth into sweet, caring kids." Sam stared straight into Max's eyes. "Are you going to miss the rest of their lives, too, the rest of your daughter's life, just because you're mad at her? Because you won't forgive her?"

"What's it to you? Are you her new boyfriend or something?" Max demanded.

"No, I'm her friend. I've seen how hard she's struggled to follow her dream, to be the mom her kids need." He paused. "My parents, my family have tried to fill in the gaps, to be the support system Joy and her children need."

"So why bother us?" The man must have a heart of stone.

"*Bother* you?" he repeated with one eyebrow arched in scornful disbelief.

"Why are you here, Sam?" Joy's mother whispered.

"Because this distance is wrong and it's gone on too long." Sam directed his comments to the weeping woman. "You're Joy's family, you are the ones she lovingly talks about when she remembers her childhood and how she learned to bake. She deserves your love."

"Butt out, okay, buddy? It's our life," Max said harshly.

"It's hers, too." Sam inhaled before adding, "Joy and her kids are living lives full of love, caring for and sharing with each other. Don't you want to be part of that? Can't you forgive whatever happened?"

"No." Max crossed his arms across his chest belligerently as his wife openly wept.

Sam knew he'd lost.

"Then I hope hanging on to your bitterness is worth missing out on the love your daughter and your grandkids could give you, Max." Sam set his card on the counter. "If you decide to fill the bread order, give me a call. Or come visit Sunshine and your family. It's up to you."

Then Sam walked out the door, mentally begging God to soften their hearts. He opened the car door and leaned in.

"There's a good restaurant down the street, guys. Let's walk there and give our legs some exercise." He held the door open as Cris and Becca tumbled out. Josh quickly joined them.

As proud as any father would be, Sam walked with the kids past their grandparents' bakery, fully aware of two sets of eyes intently following their progress. Once seated in the restaurant with their meals ordered, the two younger children asked to choose a song on the big jukebox at the front of the café. When they were gone, Josh frowned at Sam.

"That was my grandparents' bakery," he said quietly. "I remember going there once with Mom, when I was really little."

"Oh?" Sam calmly sipped his soda.

"They told us to go away. Mom said we weren't ever going back." Josh looked annoyed by Sam's calmness. "You were in there a long time just to ask directions. What are you doing, Sam?"

"Trying to make your mom's Christmas dream come true." He stared straight at Josh. "Are you going to rat me out?"

The question remained unanswered until all four of them were back in the car and heading for home.

"No," Josh murmured under cover of the two kids telling jokes in the back. "I won't tell her. Not until after Christmas anyway. But you better not hurt her or make her cry."

"I'll try not to." Sam smiled at him. "And in the meantime, would you mind praying? Hard? I think this situation is going to need some heavenly intervention."

"Doesn't everything?" Josh rolled his eyes as if to say, *Adults!*

Sam drove home trying to quell the stupid bubble of hope inside, knowing it was totally unrealistic. But maybe, just maybe, those two stubborn parents would change their minds and Joy could finally have the family Christmas she yearned for. At least *he* intended to do his utmost to facilitate a reunion for them all.

God willing.

If only Joy wouldn't hate him for interfering.

You came back with the express intent of not getting involved again, his subconscious reminded him.

But Joy was special. For her, Sam had no choice but to get involved.

Chapter Ten

On Sunday, Joy promised her kids a picnic fast-food lunch after the church service. She'd been looking forward to hearing more about building trust in God. But her ability to concentrate was severely compromised after the first hymn when Sam slipped into the seat beside her. In fact, his proximity, the piney scent of his cologne and the brush of his thumb against her hand when she passed the offering plate all distracted her so badly that by the time the pastor said the benediction, Joy could barely recall his lesson.

There had to be a way to stop Sam's effect on her, but she was so delighted to see him, she couldn't think exactly what that might be.

"Will you join me for lunch?" he invited as they moved with the crowd to the foyer.

"Mom already said we could have our lunch at the Burger Barn," Josh informed him in what Joy considered a sharp tone.

"You're very welcome to join us, if you like burgers." She sent an unspoken reprimand in her eldest son's direction.

"I love burgers. Thank you. Say, do you think the committee could borrow your kids after that?" Sam flashed his camera-loving smile at Becca and Cris. "Next week we're going to offer kids a place to make gifts for their parents, or whomever. We need to do a test run with the crafts first, hopefully with your three."

"Can we go, Mom? I only have one Christmas gift picked out." Cris looked at Sam. They shared a smile.

What was that about? Joy wondered.

"Me, too. I gotta make some gifts," Becca insisted.

Surprisingly, Josh didn't comment, which told Joy something was bothering her eldest son. She just couldn't figure out what that was.

"I guess we could try it. Let's eat first." She smiled at Sam, only then realizing that half the congregation was observing them.

Some wore funny smiles. Others nodded at each other, as if they shared some secret knowledge. Joy gulped and pretended not to see the knowing looks from people she'd only begun to befriend, though she couldn't stop blushing. She felt fairly certain the phone lines would be ringing with gossip as soon as the parishioners arrived home. She exhaled and straightened her shoulders. *Let them look.*

"Joy? Something wrong?" Sam asked.

"Not a thing. Are you riding with us to the burger joint?"

Josh opened his mouth to protest, probably irritated at the thought of losing his cherished front seat to their guest, Joy surmised. But Sam declined before her son could speak.

"Thanks but I've got some errands to run later, so I'll need my vehicle. Meet you there." He nodded then walked toward his family, swinging the youngest children in the air one by one to make them laugh. Sam would be a wonderful father.

Joy quashed the errant thought and focused on her brooding son.

Once Becca and Cris were seated inside the van, she closed the door for privacy before facing Josh.

"What's wrong with you, son? Why are you angry at Sam?"

"He's always hanging around us. He's got a big family. He doesn't need ours." Josh glared at Sam's retreating figure, yanked open the door and stepped inside the van.

"Sam has been wonderful to us," Joy chastised as she drove toward the burger place. "I expect you to give him the same courtesy we give to everyone."

"Yes, Mother." Josh sighed heavily, as if that would be an issue.

"I thought you two became friends when you started woodworking."

"That's his dad. Ben. Sam isn't very good at woodworking." Josh glared ahead for a moment then blurted, "The kids at school call Sam a liar."

"Which shows how little they know him," Joy said calmly while inside her stomach did a nosedive. "I hope you spoke up and told them how wrong they were?"

"No. I didn't."

"We don't know the details behind Sam's story," Joy warned. "He might have a very good reason for giving it. So the least we owe our friend is loyalty and understanding."

"He's not my friend." Josh didn't sound the least bit receptive to what she'd meant as a reprimand.

"Yes, he is your friend, kiddo. You just don't realize it. Who said these things about Sam anyway?" she asked, her curiosity piqued.

"A kid at school." His chin thrust out defiantly. "But everybody in town is saying it."

"Then everybody is wrong." It took only a moment for the pieces to come together. "I'm guessing you've been listening to Riley Smith. I imagine he's heard his father ranting about Sam. But they don't know the truth, son. Neither do we."

Why did it feel like she had to defend Sam?

"But—"

"Listen to me, honey. Mr. Smith has been spouting a lot of vile accusations about Sam. Mostly, I think, because he's jealous of how great Sam's ideas for the festival are turning out." She held up a hand. "No, I don't want to hear any more."

"But you don't know the truth either, Mom," Josh shot back, his tone scathing. "You just take his side because he's letting us live at the ranch."

"I trust Sam," she insisted.

"Everyone says you're in love with him. That's why you think he's so wonderful. But you don't *know* anything more about him than anybody else around town." Josh's face had turned a bright, angry red. "Sam did lie to the world. On television. That's the truth."

Everyone says you're in love with him? Oh, boy. Joy refocused.

"I *know* Sam hasn't lied to me or anyone in Sunshine since he returned, Josh. I *know* he's been very good to us. He's helped us so many times when he didn't have to."

"Lots of people have helped us," Josh snarled.

"Yes, they have. And you've never accused any of them of lying," she quietly rebuked him. "It's not Sam who bothers me right now though. At this moment I'm really ashamed that my own child can't cut our friend, a man who's been nothing but kind to him, some slack."

"Mom!" he wailed but Joy had never been so irritated with him.

"I don't care what Riley or Mr. Smith think, Josh. You're going to keep your opinions to yourself. You will be polite and respectful to Sam."

"But—" She didn't let him continue.

"Hear me well, Josh. When he's ready, Sam will explain why he gave that story," Joy said firmly. "Or maybe he won't. Either way, this family is going to trust him, because he deserves it. Do you understand me?"

Several minutes passed before Josh finally nodded. "Yes," he grumbled.

"Good. Now let's go and enjoy our lunch, *with our friend*." As Joy turned into the parking lot, she was shocked by how many cars filled it.

"I hope we can find a seat," Sam said, joining them. "Looks pretty busy."

"They come to Sunshine even on Sunday, when our stores are closed?" Joy marveled. "It's quite amazing, this Experience Christmas festival you've created."

"We," Sam corrected. "What this community has created. And yes, it is."

"I don't care if it's full inside. It's nice out. I want to eat out here," Josh said without looking at her. "So do Becca and Cris. We'll wait at this picnic table."

"Okay." Joy wasn't about to argue. She figured a little time-out was a good thing for both of them. "Let's go order, Sam."

It took more than half an hour to get their food. When at last they carried it outside, they found all three kids staring at the open field that lay just outside of town. Joy followed their gaze and blinked.

"What is that?" she asked.

"Wind skiing. Or some might call it kite skiing." Sam

explained, "The skier uses a kite to harness the wind. That gives them power over bumps or to jump. The kite makes it possible for the person to travel on their skis, up or downhill, with any wind direction."

"Was it expensive to bring that display in?" she murmured, pondering that loan for the community hall. Sam would be on the hook if it wasn't repaid by Christmas.

"Cost to us? Zero." Sam grinned at her surprise. "A company in Missoula heard how many people were attending our festival. They offered to bring some boards and kites for demonstration with the agreement that kids and adults could try them out. Since they assume all liability and it's outside of Sunshine's town limits, the committee approved."

"They sure have a great turnout." Joy tried and failed to count the total number of skiers gliding across the snow.

"Have you ever kite skied, Sam?" Josh's longing gaze was riveted on the big colorful sails.

"A couple of times in Switzerland on snow and once on sand in the Sahara. It's really easy. Maybe you can try it later?" Sam glanced at Joy, his expression questioning.

"But I want to make Cwismas gifts," Becca protested.

"I want to do both," Cris countered.

"Let's eat our lunch first," Joy said with a chuckle. "Then I'll take Becca and Cris to the Christmas gift-making class. Josh, perhaps if you ask nicely, Sam will go with you to try the kites. Or skis. Or whatever."

"You don't want to try?" Sam waved a hand at the kites, one eyebrow arched in inquiry.

"I'll pass this time, thanks. Though it does look fun." Joy chewed her burger while watching the skiers zoom across the pristine snow. "It seems effortless. Perfect weather for it, too, with this light breeze."

When they'd finished lunch, Sam walked with them to the community hall.

"You really don't want to go skiing?" His dark eyes held hers, as if he somehow understood her unspoken but overwhelming yearning to get away, relinquish her cares for a little while, and let the massive sail grab an air current and carry her up and away. "I'd be there to help you."

"It's very nice of you to offer," she murmured, tearing her gaze from his. "I want to spend some time with these two, but I would appreciate it if you'd watch out for Josh."

"Mom!" her eldest protested.

"You can't try it if there's no adult supervision. That's one of the stipulations." Sam studied Josh. "How about this? You can practice while the others do crafts. Then I'll text your mom so she, Becca and Cris can come watch you."

"Great idea!" Joy said, sloughing off her anxiety about her child's safety. "Be careful. And listen to Sam!" she called to Josh, who was already walking away.

"He'll be fine." Sam's hand covered hers, squeezed it and then dropped away. "Have fun making gifts. By the way, I need a new tie."

"You don't wear ties, Sam," Cris protested.

"True." He laughed before hurrying after Josh. "Wait up, buddy."

"Can we go inside now?" Becca begged.

"Sure." Joy helped them off with their coats and on with big aprons that covered their church clothes.

"Hi there, Joy. Hey, kids. Come on, I'll show you what we're offering today." Bonnie led them around the big hall, pointing out areas for decorating plaster of paris Christmas plaques, making macramé hangings and even indicated a stall for making snow globes.

There were lots more crafts on offer, but Becca preferred the plaques while Cris wanted to make snow globes. They paused once to go watch Josh kite ski, and then returned, eager to complete a second and then a third craft.

"What are you going to do with so many gifts?" Joy wondered.

"I dunno." Becca shrugged. "But on TV they said you can't have too many gifts."

"Honey, that's not—"

"Let them do more, Joy," Bonnie urged. "Their work really helps us figure out areas where we need to rethink the projects."

"But you can't watch me now, Mommy," Becca insisted.

"Not me, neither," Cris agreed.

"Why not?" Joy asked.

"'Cause we might be makin' *your* gift," Cris explained. Becca nodded. Their eyes sparkled with excitement as they grinned at each other.

Joy felt a rush of happiness well inside. Her kids truly were "experiencing Christmas."

"There are coffee and snacks over in the corner," Sam's mom advised with a wink. "Why don't you relax while these munchkins work. We have plenty of helpers."

"Okay, I will. Thank you." Joy found a quiet corner and studied her phone, checking her plans for the upcoming week.

Her orders were in. Her staff was scheduled. The only thing she hadn't been able to accomplish was finding a new bread supplier. Complaints about their current one were mounting due to stale bread and improperly baked loaves. Joy hated the negativity her bakery was receiving because of someone else's poor quality control.

As usual, thoughts filled her head of her parents' bakery and the hours of playtime she'd spent as a child at a little table in the back, making stars and trees and then decorating them for Christmas. How important she'd felt.

Then, as she grew up, she'd been given more tasks in the bakery itself until finally she'd worked alongside her dad, proudly producing their signature bread and other delicacies, some of them her own recipes. Her parents had even taken a short holiday one summer and left her in charge. By the next summer, though, it was all over. They'd kicked her out. A wash of loneliness swamped Joy.

If only she could talk to her parents—*Why not phone them?* They would probably refuse to talk to her, but if there was even a chance to heal the breach between them, she had to take it. For her kids' sake. To give them the family Christmas she yearned for. Joy dialed the number from memory.

"Hi, Mom." She inhaled and silently prayed for courage. "How are you?"

"Joy, your father says I'm not to talk to you." The whisper stabbed Joy's heart worse than a knife.

"But we're just talking. We're not doing anything. Are you all right, Mom? You sound funny."

"I've got a cold." That explained the raspy sound. Maybe. Or was her mom ill? How Joy hated this distance between them.

"I won't talk long, Mom. It's just—I was wondering. Do you think the kids and I could see you?" she asked tentatively. "I hate that they don't know their grandparents. I think you'd like them," she added in a broken whisper.

"Who is that?" a voice demanded.

"Joy. She wants to meet." Her mother's voice seemed to shrink into nothingness as she handed over the phone.

"Why do you keep hounding us?" her father's voice boomed in her ear. "You made your choice. You married that good-for-nothing loser despite my objections. So he left you penniless and alone with three kids. That's not our fault. You're getting exactly what you chose."

"I know. But please, Dad. I'd like to put the past behind us. I want us to be a family again," she said desperately. "Your grandchildren—"

"Stop bothering us. We're going on with our life. You do the same."

The line went dead before she could utter another word. Joy couldn't help it. Tears flowed down her cheeks.

"Joy?" Sam asked, his arm sliding across her shoulders. "What on earth is wrong?"

Sam was glad Josh was in deep discussion with a skier outside. Becca and Cris were also busily engaged in snacking at the moment, which left Sam free to comfort Joy.

"Talk to me," he murmured.

"I called my parents." She slid her phone into her handbag with a sniff. "I asked Mom if we could get together so they could meet their grandchildren. Then Dad took the phone." She laughed, but her voice wobbled as she said, "Let's just say that didn't go well."

Her feeble attempt at mirth told Sam exactly how badly it had gone.

"I'm so sorry," he murmured, squeezing her shoulder and then brushing the tears from her cheeks.

"How can my father be so bitter after all this time?" she whispered. "It's not the kids' faults that I made a mistake."

"You were just a kid, too," he reminded her.

"I was, but I should have listened to them. I should

have done as they asked. I've made so many mistakes," she said sadly.

"Joy, we all make mistakes. It's how we learn." He risked saying what he thought she *needed* to hear. "Your parents are making a mistake, too, in missing out on your kids' lives. I suppose they think they're punishing you, but in reality it's them who are punishing themselves. Unforgiveness is a rock that causes a lot of damage. Trust me, I know."

"What do you mean?" Joy frowned.

"It took me a really long time to let go of my anger and, all right, *hatred* of the men who kidnapped Celia, the men who locked her in a damp cell but wouldn't get her inhaler. Those men caused her death."

"Oh, Sam."

He shrugged at her dismayed expression, his hand spreading over hers like a shield.

"I hated them so badly I couldn't do my job. I had to take time off to come home to the ranch and let God heal my soul. My parents helped, too."

"You must have loved her very much," Joy whispered.

"I did, but it wasn't just losing Celia that caused me problems. It was the anger and hate festering inside. It should have been directed at myself. I was to blame. Instead I targeted God with my unhappiness and anger." He grimaced but admitted the truth. "I've had to deal with those feelings all over again since my latest trip to the Middle East."

"Because?" That was Joy, always probing deeper for the truth.

"Because I felt abandoned, as if God didn't care about me or what was happening to me." Sam sighed. "It sounds awful to admit this, but I think I almost hated God for what I went through, what I'm still going through."

"The PTSD," she murmured.

"And the nightmares. And the cold sweats, and the worry and the fear that I'm not the man I was," he admitted ruefully. "I've lost my confidence, my swagger as some friends used to call it. I've also lost my friends. Doing what I thought was right cost me all of it."

"I'm so sorry, Sam." She brushed his cheek with her free hand. "I know about lost confidence. I've always felt I was a mistake waiting to happen. I've certainly made enough of them in my life."

"I don't think anything you do is a mistake, Joy," Sam said, and meant it.

"That's nice of you, but it is *not* what I have believed for so many years. I thought everything I saw or touched or did was wrong, that God had created a mistake in me." She forced a smile and a laugh.

"But you don't feel that way now?"

"Sometimes I do," she admitted. "But since I've been doing a Bible study with Grace, I've begun to understand that God doesn't make mistakes. Each problem or trial I go through is like a steppingstone to a place He's taking me." She scrunched up her face. "It sounds easy when I say it like that, but it isn't easy at all."

"So how do you do it?" Sam loved that she hadn't moved away from him, that she was sharing her most personal issues with him. With Joy, he wasn't a liar. With Joy he could just be Sam. He treasured that. "What's your secret?"

"No secret. I just keep on walking, even though I often stumble. When I do, Grace is teaching me to trust that God will help me reach the next stone." She sighed. "But I've had to learn that even if I misstep, He is still there with me, and He will hold me and keep me from anything He doesn't want me to have. *Trust* is becoming my favorite word." When Joy lifted her head, her silky curls brushed his chin.

"It is? Why?" he asked as she shifted from under his arm, putting a distance between them.

"Hmm. I'm not sure I can explain this properly," she said earnestly. "What I'm trying to say is that finding self-confidence isn't some big mystery I have to solve. It's a daily choice to trust God to make me who He wants me to be. It's faith," she said simply.

"I think you're amazing." Sam admired this woman more than he'd ever admired anyone.

He wanted so badly to kiss her. But there were too many people around, not the least of whom were his mother and Josh. Not only that, but he had nothing to offer Joy. No job, not even his reputation. The truth wasn't yet out there, and when it was, he had no idea how she'd react to it.

The other reason he couldn't kiss her was that to Joy, a kiss would have meaning. Promise. Joy didn't flirt. She was sweet and, despite being the mother of three kids, innocent. If she gave love, she'd give it willingly. Sam couldn't toy with her emotions, especially not when he wasn't yet sure of his own feelings. Or his faith.

"Actually, Sam," she said, her smile reappearing like a rainbow after a storm, "I'm certain you haven't lost anything. Certainly not your *swagger* and not your friends. At least not this friend."

"Thank you, Joy," he said simply.

"Welcome." She was looking at him in a way that made his stomach do flip-flops.

"What else did your parents have to say when you called?" Sam intentionally broke the quiet intimacy that had grown between them. He had to. It had become too intense, adding to his longing to embrace her.

"It was strange." Joy frowned. "Dad asked me to *stop* hounding them. But I haven't even spoken to them since Josh was a little guy." She shrugged then pointed. "Look. There's Miss Partridge. I think that boy she brought in is in Becca's class. He looks really upset!"

"Let's go see if we can help." He rose and held out his hand, but not simply because he wanted them to help a needy child.

Sam needed space from Joy. He needed time to figure out whether he was ready to get involved in a serious relationship again. He'd avoided that for so long, kept his heart chained so he could never be so overwhelmed by loss again. But for Joy, nothing more than giving his whole heart would do. And he couldn't do that because he wasn't free to. Not yet.

The very last thing Sam wanted to do was hurt this special woman. So it was better to maintain his distance until he thought things through and got free of his entanglements. He just hoped his willpower was strong enough to last that long!

After a second glimpse, Sam recognized the boy with Miss Partridge. Trent Scott. He also knew the family. They were desperately poor. Since learning Trent's father had lost his job two weeks ago, Sam had recommended him for several odd jobs with different retailers in town. He'd also sent a couple of gift cards anonymously to help feed the family.

Now he listened with Joy as Miss Partridge explained sotto voce that she'd hired Trent to clean her snow-covered sidewalks so he'd have money to buy his parents gifts. Instead Trent had selflessly given his earnings to his parents to pay for a needed repair on their car.

"So he's suddenly realized he has no way to buy them

Christmas presents," she said. "That's why I brought him here."

"Great idea." Sam tried hard to interest Trent in several crafts other kids were making, but when nothing seemed to speak to Trent, he called his mother over for help.

"Oh, I know the perfect thing," Bonnie said, patting his cheek, though Trent eased away, obviously feeling he was too old for such treatment. "Your mom loves flowers, right, Trent? Well, we haven't actually set this station up yet. It will have these little pottery vases you can paint. If you glue a hook on the back, it will hang on the wall. Then you can tuck a bunch of dried flowers in them. Or fresh ones, if you prefer. Would you like to be the first person to try this craft? Do you think she'd like it?"

"Yes." Trent immediately set to work, putting some very fine details into his painting.

When he was finished, Bonnie praised him for his excellent work and then suggested he make a memory book for his dad, drawing pictures with descriptions beneath of all the fun things they'd done together. Trent loved the idea and spent a long time creating his book.

When he was finished, Joy helped him wrap and label both gifts while her own kids finished up their crafts. Ben said he needed some exercise and would walk home with Trent. Sam suspected his dad would offer some work for Trent's dad. It made him smile that his kind father couldn't stand to see a man wanting. Ben would figure out a way to step in without being obvious.

"Wasn't that just the biggest blessing the Lord could give us this afternoon?" Bonnie gushed as Ben and Trent left. "What parent can resist a child's handmade gift? They just melt your heart."

A lightbulb went off in Sam's brain.

Maybe Joy's parents wouldn't be able to resist if their grandchildren sent them special handmade Christmas gifts. The tricky part would be to do it without telling Joy. Then, if nothing came of it, she wouldn't be hurt.

And if something did? Sam recalled her words about trust.

So I think I have to trust You to work this out for Joy and her kids, he prayed as he left the hall to run his errands. *You're in charge. Of everything.*

He glanced at the burner phone vibrating on his console. A message flashed.

Christmas.

Nothing would happen until Christmas? But it had already been so long.

A deep weariness threatened to overwhelm Sam. Would it ever really be over? Would his sacrifice in that dark, dank place be enough? Would his source finally be safe next week, or would Sam have to keep quiet even longer?

Trust *is my favorite word*, Joy had said.

"Can You help me make it my favorite word, too?" he prayed. "Can You help me trust, if only until Christmas?"

Chapter Eleven

"Uh, Joy? Could you please come back here?"

Surprised that Clara would call her to the back on a very busy Tuesday morning, Joy excused herself from the front and hurried to see what her head baker needed. She gaped at the stacks of bread standing on their loading dock. She didn't need to look twice to recognize the logo from her parents' bakery.

"Where did this come from? What is going on?"

"Don't ask me. I just work here." Clara spread her hands, palms upward. "I opened the door and there it was on the dock. Waiting." She shrugged. "However it happened, I sure am glad we won't have to carry that awful Montana's Best Bread anymore. At least not according to this." She pulled off an invoice that was taped to the top of one stack. "It says *daily* deliveries."

"Daily? Then I guess I'd better cancel all future orders with Montana's." Joy studied the invoice, unable to make the pieces fit.

Why had her parents had their bread delivered here? How had they known where she was, never mind that she'd opened this bakery?

Joy pulled out her phone and dialed her parents' number, but her call was forwarded to their answering machine. Frustrated, she didn't leave a message. She needed to talk to them in person, to find out why her father had sent this bread. Because she knew beyond a shadow of a doubt that he *had* done this.

"You're needed up front, Joy." Clara pushed one of the stacks of bread toward her. "Take these with you to sell."

"It's a good thing there are less than two weeks until Christmas," Joy muttered to herself as she rolled the bread to the front of the store. "Given the pace at which things keep happening around here, I need a break."

But in her heart she was praising God. Another prayer answered. And this time, she wouldn't have to refund any money. Her parents' bread was the best.

With a nudge from her staff, Joy took an hour off after lunch to wander the streets and soak in the festive atmosphere. It seemed that every time she turned around, she saw Sam, meeting and greeting visitors, directing events and always, always smiling.

"You're like Sunshine's goodwill ambassador," she told him when he eventually spotted her and came over to talk. "These crowds are amazing for a Tuesday."

"Today's crowds are due to the gingerbread contest. We keep repeating it and people keep entering, so this time we scheduled it for a Tuesday afternoon." He chuckled. "No kids entered, but two busloads of seniors have already shown up with word of another bus on the way. Better bake another batch."

"Way ahead of you," Joy told him, feeling smugly complacent. "Clara knocked off two big gingerbread bakes before we opened this morning. So there. Bring it, Sam!" She beckoned him with both hands, grinning. "We're ready."

"You sound like the teens I've been working with," he complained. "They constantly tell me to *bring it*."

"Not that you need any encouragement in that vein," she teased, glancing around. "I think you've already *brought it* admirably. Now I'd better get back to work. I have three cakes to decorate for some birthday celebrations happening tonight, after the town square Christmas tree lighting."

"You're coming, aren't you? The carpentry class from the high school is putting up a huge nativity scene in the trees with special lights and music." Sam ticked events off on his fingertips. "We'll also have a fire, and we'll roast wieners and marshmallows for s'mores and…"

"Sam, stop." Joy touched his arm, trying not to laugh. "I *know*. I live here. I have your posters in my shop." She did laugh when he got a very self-conscious look on his face. "I'll be there, providing Josh has his homework done."

"He will." His smug expression bugged her.

"How do you know that?" she demanded, wondering if this was another of those *coincidences* that seemed to follow him.

"I probably shouldn't tell you this, but I think you should be prepared." Sam leaned so close his minty breath grazed across her face. "Josh is going to ask if he can be your salesman tonight."

"He's too young," Joy objected. Then curiosity grew. "Selling what?"

"Whatever you give him, I guess. Cookies, fudge. Popcorn?" Sam shrugged, but the way he'd added *popcorn* told her he had an idea.

"Popcorn?" She frowned. "I run a bakery, Sam."

"Uh-huh." He crossed his arms over his chest and nodded.

"Popcorn is not a baked item."

"It could be." He met her frown head-on.

"Just to be clear—you want me to make popcorn and put it into little bags for my son to wander around selling tonight." She didn't get it. "Why, exactly, would I do that?"

"So Josh can earn money. The church intends to take the Sunday-school kids for a day trip to the mountains in January. Josh wants to go. He wants to earn money to pay for kite-skiing lessons."

"Oh." How could she argue with her son taking on that kind of responsibility? "But popcorn?"

"Well, you see, Mrs. Baker, folks around here aren't real crazy about chestnuts, even *if* they're roasted over an open fire." Sam paused to smile and wave at someone, and then resumed his explanation. "But let's say you took popcorn and pretzels and some mixed nuts. And let's say you covered them all with a caramel syrup and baked it for a while until it all stuck together."

"Okay," she said as he licked his lips.

"Well, I think that could be a real good bakery treat, especially if it's sold warm. I'd buy it." This little speech was followed by a wink that made her knees weak.

Joy shook her head. This was Sam at his best, chock-full of inventive ideas, even for a young boy who wanted to earn some pocket money. Lost his swagger indeed! Hardly.

"I even thought of a name."

"Do tell." She waited for it, certain it would be a good name given his excited expression.

"Ticklebellies." He laughed at her surprise. "It fits. Josh could do pretty well selling Ticklebellies, I think."

"Where *do* you get these ideas from, Sam?" Joy pretended to glare at him. "And why do *your* ideas always involve so much work for *me*?"

"Just the way it is, Mrs. Baker." He grinned unrepentantly. "Brains and brawn. No, wait. That doesn't work." His frown made Joy burst into laughter.

"You're incorrigible."

"By the way, Josh and Dad have already made a little wooden box and painted it with red and white stripes," Sam said smoothly. "And Mom made a strap that can hang around Josh's neck to hold his Ticklebellies. If you heated some stones or something in that oven of yours, they should keep his popcorn warm while he sells it."

"So your parents are in on this scheme, too?" Joy couldn't help smiling. Sam was like no other man she'd ever met.

"Didn't hear it from me." Sam assumed his innocent look, which was not very convincing. "Gotta get back to work. I haven't checked the Christmas tree lights yet, and Miss P.'s supposed to talk to me about something, too."

"Say, about Grace." Joy glanced around to make sure the lady wasn't nearby to overhear. "Did you know that she's looking for love?"

"Looking—" Sam's eyes widened to huge brown orbs. "No, I did not know that." He blinked. "And I *need* to know this why, exactly?"

"Well, because you're out here with all these people, all the time," Joy said, surprised he couldn't see the reason for himself. "You meet and greet and learn things about who's who all the time."

"Uh-huh." When he still looked confused, Joy got to the point.

"Given all your interactions, I thought maybe you could come up with a candidate for her. Someone special, not necessarily from around here, but mature and interesting and good-looking. She really wants a chance to be in love, Sam."

"Ah." He frowned, head tipped slightly to one side. "Why is this so important to you, Joy?"

"Because she's done so much for me. She's the reason I became a Christian and she's patiently taught me about it, answering my many questions so kindly." A little embarrassed by her fervor, Joy pressed on anyway. "Grace feels alone. She really wants someone in her life, someone to love."

"I don't know," Sam said dubiously. "Me matchmaking?"

"Not that. Just keeping your eyes open," Joy corrected him. "Love would give Grace someone with whom to share her world, a companion. You know how she always talks about traveling. Love could be fantastic for Grace Partridge."

"But love also brings pain and loss." Sam's expression turned blank now. "It's not all chocolates and roses."

"Would you prefer to have done without the love you and Celia shared if it meant you could escape the pain of losing her?" Joy demanded.

"Would you want to do without the love you had for Nick if it meant you'd escape all those mistakes you keep claiming you made?" he shot back.

Joy thought for a moment and then shook her head. "No. Never."

"What?" Sam looked flabbergasted by her response. "Why?"

"Because love *can be* wonderful," she said softly. "Our love, even if it wasn't very long-lasting, even though it wasn't what I hoped or expected, gave me three wonderful children who fill my life with joy every single time they smile."

"Oh." He frowned at her uncertainly.

"Yes, I suffered. But for the rest of my life I'll have my kids to love and cherish. That's worth taking a risk on love and on getting hurt, Sam. Gotta go." She fluttered her fingers. "See you tonight."

It was only when she was back at the bakery, popping a huge kettle of corn, that Joy realized she hadn't told Sam about the bread delivery. And she wasn't going to, she decided as she stirred the caramel syrup. Sam had enough to do with the town's festivities. People dumped problems on him all day long.

When the two of them had a few minutes together, he deserved to forget about all issues, hers included. Joy would keep this to herself while she praised God for answered prayer.

But then a curious thought teased her. Sam couldn't have had anything to do with the bread. Could he? That was silly. He didn't even know her parents!

Joy forgot the questions as she tossed her popcorn mixture. She filled small white bags that had *Joy's Treats* written in neat black script with the mouth-watering mixture, rolled the tops closed and placed the bags in a warmer.

But no matter how busy she kept, concerns about Sam kept bubbling up.

I'm being as suspicious as Evan Smith, she chastised herself. *Sam's a good guy, but even he doesn't have enough persuasiveness to break through Dad's stubbornness.*

Joy faced facts. Every time she was near Sam, and often even from a distance, his magnetic personality drew her closer. She enjoyed being with him, doing things with him, talking to him.

Despite her comment to Sam about Nick, however, she still carried mental scars from loving and being hurt.

"Sam's just a really good friend," she assured herself.

"Sure wish I had a *good* friend like that." Grace Partridge stood behind her, smiling as if the two of them shared a secret. "I think you love Sam, Joy."

Loved him?

She couldn't. Could she?

Joy had to sit down.

Sam's shoulder nudged Joy's to watch Josh peddle his Ticklebellies.

"Your son is a very good salesman."

"So are you." She indicated the hot dog in her hands. "I'm not terribly fond of these, you know, and yet here I am eating one. Because of your persuasiveness."

"Come on!" Sam pretended astonishment. "Fresh buns from our local bakery. Meat that's carefully charred to a crisp over a campfire. Oodles of relish and mustard. What's not to like?" He leaned forward and dabbed something from the corner of her lips. "When you finish that, I'll buy you a hot chocolate," he promised with a grin.

"*Buy* me? It's free!" Joy was having fun. For this one night, she wasn't going to worry about defining their relationship. It was enough just to be here with Sam, enjoy the evening and his company and experience the Christmas tree lighting together.

"Oh, oh. Miss P. is beckoning. I guess that's my cue to get onstage." Sam stared at her. "Is my face clean?"

"Mostly." Joy laughed at his glare. "You look great."

"Thanks. So do you." His brown eyes held hers like a magnet as he leaned closer.

Close enough to kiss? Her heart kicked into high gear.

Then someone bumped Joy's arm and Sam stepped out of the way of the condiments spilling from her hot dog. The expression on his face grew rueful, as if he'd regretted getting too close.

"I'll be back in a minute."

"I'll be here." She watched him go, sorry that he couldn't have even one night off, and yet thrilled that they would still have some time during this evening to spend together. Sam was an awesome man. He was definitely another of the blessings God had been sending her way lately.

"Ladies, gentlemen and kids of all ages. Welcome to Experience Christmas. Again," Sam said wryly. Everyone laughed. "Tonight we're gathered to light Sunshine's main Christmas tree. It's a tradition that's been carried on for generations in our town. Every year we turn off all the lights for a few minutes so we can truly appreciate our Christmas tree. That will happen right away." Sam seemed confused as Miss Partridge handed him a note. "But, uh, first, our mayor has something to say."

"Thank you, Sam." The mayor gazed out at the crowd for a second.

Joy wondered what was happening.

"Tonight I am pleased to announce that the town of Sunshine has completely paid off our loan on the community center."

Amid wild cheers and furious applause, it took a few moments to settle everyone down. Once there was quiet, the mayor continued.

"We are especially delighted to share this news as an invitation to you and anyone you wish to bring along, to join us in celebration at Sunshine's annual potluck supper on Christmas Eve, at our community center. Everyone is welcome. The more the merrier."

The park exploded with cheers all over again.

Joy couldn't smother her own giddy relief. Sam had

done it. Whatever money came in now could be used for other needed community projects, but better than that, Sam was off the hook for that big loan.

"I think this is going to be the best Christmas ever," Miss Partridge said in her ear.

"I think so, too." Joy hugged her then sobered. "It won't be exactly the kind of family Christmas I wanted to give the kids, but—"

"It can be, Joy. Families are made up of people you love. So are family Christmases. Look around. Isn't there anyone here you love?" Grace leaned closer to whisper, "Don't you care for Sam?"

Yes. Yes, she did. Joy stood silent, letting the warm feelings flood her insides. She cared for him a great deal. She wanted to see him succeed beyond anyone's wildest expectations. But did loving him mean she'd have to give up her determination to stand on her own two feet, to let go of her independence and her dreams?

Bemused by her thoughts, Joy watched the streetlights blink off as the Christmas tree lights came on, their many colors illuminating the area in a warm, loving glow. And then Sam was there, his arm curving around her waist.

At his touch, Joy felt her heart light up like the Christmas lights. In the very depths of her being, she cared deeply for this man. It seemed totally natural to rest her head on Sam's shoulder and join in as the mayor led everyone in singing "Silent Night." There were more carols, happy ones, thoughtful ones. People moved and shifted, smiling at each other as they shared the beauty of time spent together.

Amid the shuffling and singing, Joy and Sam ended up at the back of the crowd, beside the stand of massive evergreens that bounded this side of the park. Joy spotted her kids with Grace, staring at the massive Christmas tree as they munched on Ticklebellies between carols. Joy had no doubt Grace had bought out the last of Josh's supply.

"Are you cold, Joy?"

"No." She twisted to face Sam, loving the way he looked at her as if there was nothing he wanted to change about her, as if it didn't matter that she'd messed up so many times in her life. "I'm just fine."

"Yes, you are," he agreed solemnly. "You're also very beautiful. I've been wanting to do this for so long." He bent his head and kissed her, tenderly, the lightest of touches, his lips barely grazing hers, as if she was the most delicate, precious thing in his world. As if she was a treasure he valued.

Joy got lost in that kiss, in the feelings that filled her—joy, happiness, wonder, delight. When Sam drew back after several blissful moments, she whimpered, not wanting this bliss to end. So she slid her arms around his neck and drew his lips against hers once more, trying to tell him wordlessly something she didn't really understand, because she'd never felt like this before.

Her heart throbbed with delight at his embrace. Her soul sang with joy that this wonderful, caring man saw something he liked in her.

"Joy. What a fitting name you have. I love your curls," he whispered, spreading his fingers through them. "They're soft and sweet, just like you. Sturdy yet strong. You push ahead, beat down the obstacles and make things happen. I love that about you."

Love? Joy blinked at him, confused by what he'd said. It was too soon. And yet, his brown eyes met hers openly, without shadows. How could she have any doubts?

"I care about you very much, Joy," Sam said as his thumb traced her mouth. "I think I have since the first day I saw you wearing that ridiculous hat. You were so annoyed at Dad and me, and the tree most of all."

"Sam, I—"

He shushed her, chuckling at her indignant face before pressing a kiss against her jaw. Then he leaned away from her as his eyes searched hers.

"You kiss me as if you understand how I feel. You kiss me the way I've wanted you to for so long." His breath burst out in a white cloud. "But I still don't dare believe it."

"Believe what, Sam?" she whispered, afraid she knew what his question was and not prepared to give the answer she thought he wanted.

"That you might love me." His voice rasped with insecurity. "Or if not love, then care just a little about me."

"That hardly expresses how I feel," she said with a smile. "You're the very best friend I've ever had, Sam. I love the way you step in and fill a need no matter what it is. I love your heart for this community and the people in it. I love how you care for me and for my kids. And I love that you're God-focused. That you're trying to make Him an even bigger part of your life."

"Really?" Sam stared. "You feel all that?"

"Of course." Joy pressed a kiss against each cheek. "But I don't know if I love you."

"Oh." He gulped.

"I'm sorry, but that's the truth. I feel like everything between us has happened so fast that I need time to absorb it, to make sense of it."

"Okay."

"That's all you're going to say?" she asked, nestling just a little closer.

"What were you hoping for? Four calling birds? Three French hens? Two turtle doves?" He was teasing her now.

She could tell by a tiny tic at the corner of his mouth that he was trying to break the solemnness of the moment. Because he was afraid, like she was?

"No, none of those. Maybe I was hoping for some clarity. Maybe more of this would, um, *bring it*." She kissed him on the lips, smothering his groan while thrilling to his touch and wishing it would clear up the confusion in her brain.

"You're not helping *me* gain clarity, Joy." Sam sounded like he was gasping for air. "We have to stop this."

She trailed her fingers over his broad shoulders. "Why?"

"Because your kids are coming." Sam gently set her away from him, but not before he cupped her cheeks in his palms for a few wonderful moments. "I do care about you," he whispered.

"I care about you, too," she repeated, afraid to say more. She'd made an awful mistake saying that to Nick. What if this feeling she had was a mistake, too? A mirage that wasn't what it seemed?

"Mom?" Josh called.

"Yes. We're over here." She smiled when the three children appeared. "Hi."

"What are you doing here?" Josh asked.

"Looking at the Christmas tree lights and the nativity scene over there," she said, though she'd only just noticed the display mere moments before. "How did the popcorn sell?"

"Great! I made almost a hundred dollars." Her son went on to explain the sales pitch he'd employed, adding, "I want to try it again before Christmas."

"Sure." Joy realized Sam was drawing them from the little glade without appearing to steer anyone. She was glad. She needed to gain some perspective, at least until she figured out her own mind.

"I'm tired, Mommy." Cris took her hand and yawned.

Joy checked the town clock and gasped.

"Later than you thought, huh?" Sam said with a secret smile meant just for her.

"Much later. Come along, children. Time to go home. Wasn't it a wonderful night?"

They all agreed it had been great. Sam walked them to the bakery, where Joy's van sat out front. Once the kids were belted in, he held her door and just stared, as if he was memorizing her features.

"Are you coming, Mom?" Josh asked.

"Yes. I'm coming." She smiled at Sam and whispered, "See you tomorrow."

"Bright and early," he said seriously, his smile dissipating. "I need to talk to you, Joy."

"Good. Because I need to talk to you, too." She squeezed his hand then got into her van. "Good night, Sam."

"Good night, Joy. Good night, kids."

Sam closed the door and stood on the sidewalk, watching as she drove away. Joy thought he looked troubled, but then her rear window was fogging up and she couldn't see very clearly as the distance yawned.

Once the kids were tucked in bed, Joy sank into her favorite chair in front of the window and relived every wonderful second of those stolen moments under the snow-laden spruce bough.

"You created a wonderful thing when You created love, God," she whispered, her spirit lighter than it had been for years. "But I can't tell if love is what I feel for Sam. If it is, it would be the most wonderful Christmas gift, but I need You to help me lest I make another mistake."

Still, despite her doubts, a teasing thought fluttered in the back of her brain.

Maybe a family Christmas wasn't out of the question.

It was time to tell Joy the truth.

Sam had spent the night tossing and turning, trying to fight what he knew he had to do. But there was no getting around it. His dishonesty with her had preyed on his mind for too long. And why? Because he feared that if she knew what he'd done, both in the Middle East and in Sunshine, Joy wouldn't speak to him anymore. She was so proud of her success, proud that she'd managed to achieve her dream on her own. Telling her the truth could crush her.

Sam had spent hours after his Bible study with his dad, trying to wriggle out of it. But it didn't take a voice from Heaven to know God expected him to tell the truth. Ben would say the same. Hadn't he urged Sam over and over to trust his heavenly Father to work out his issues? Sam had been skittering around trust for too long. It was time to grab hold of his faith and just do it.

God had worked things out so far. True, Sam still didn't have a concrete resolution for his source overseas. But at least there'd been some movement. They'd texted *Christmas*. That meant something was happening. When it did, Sam wanted Joy to be prepared, to know the truth about him and what he'd done. He cared deeply about her. He didn't want her blindsided or confused and uncertain, because of him.

After a night of thinking it over, Sam was positive he loved Joy. He hadn't wanted to fall in love, hadn't wanted to leave himself open to pain and heartache, to loss. He was afraid to commit. But there it was. He loved her. The certainty in his heart didn't waver, even in light of the monumental task he faced.

When you loved someone, you owed them the truth. No matter what.

At 4:00 a.m., Sam rose and prepared for his day. He spent some time in prayer, not sure exactly what he should ask for but finally yielding it all to God to work out. He kept wanting to take it back, to try to figure out a new way, but he understood now that it would take time and repeated relinquishing of control to gain the trust he wanted to have. God was patient, his dad had said. God didn't give up on His children just because they were slow learners.

In Sunshine, Sam saw no one on the streets. It was far too early for that. The lights in the bakery were on, though, and Joy's van was parked in its usual spot at the side. In fact, he'd heard her van leaving the ranch earlier. He'd let her go, figuring it would be easier to talk to her here, at the bakery, before the day's rush began.

He ached to hold her in his arms, to keep her captive if she wanted to leave after he'd opened his heart. But it would be her choice. Sam had never been so aware that with one confession he could lose everything he now realized he desperately wanted.

"Help me, God."

The east door was open because Clara accessed the garbage bins that way. Sam stepped inside. He took moved silently around the walk-in freezer and stopped, dismay billowing inside him at what he saw. Max Coyne was here? He was delivering his own bread today?

"I don't understand what changed, Dad," Joy said, her back to Sam. "Why did you suddenly decide to supply me with bread?"

"We did it because of him." Max pointed to Sam.

Joy swiveled. She smiled when she saw him. Then she faced her dad again. "Sam? What has Sam got to do with you bringing me your bread?"

"He insisted we had to let you sell our bread or your bakery would fail."

"I never said that!" Sam glared at Joy's father.

"Close enough." Max turned to the door. "I have to go."

"Thank you for the bread, Dad," Joy said in an almost whisper. "I'll send you a check."

Max nodded and left via the loading dock.

"Joy, it isn't how he said." Sam stopped. Her face was whiter than he'd ever seen it. She wouldn't look at him but instead walked across the floor toward a room marked *Office*.

"We'll talk here, in private, so Clara can't hear." Her usually lilting voice sounded colder than any ice sculpture. "I want the truth, Sam. All of it. Now."

Sam followed, closed the door quietly and faced her.

"No lies. No pretense. Just the truth."

"Yes. That's why I came here this morning. The day I took the kids…" he began. Her lips tightened. "We stopped at your parents' bakery. I went in. The kids stayed in the car."

"Why?" That one word sounded like the keening cry of an animal who'd been abandoned. Sam hated it.

"Because I want you to have your family Christmas. I want them to forgive and forget," he said, meeting her glacial green gaze. "I wanted them to meet your kids, to love them and you. To be the kind of support you, Josh, Becca and Cris need. I thought maybe I could help make that happen."

One look at her cold expression told Sam he'd just blown his chances with Joy. She'd needed only one thing from him and he'd broken it.

Trust.

Chapter Twelve

"I'm sorry, but I don't think that's the truth, Sam."

Joy watched his shoulders sag and knew her words had hurt him deeply. She regretted saying them, but she was hurting, too.

"It is the truth," he insisted. "I wanted the best for you. Because I love you."

"Love doesn't go behind someone's back. Love doesn't lie." Every part of her heart ached as the truth sank in. "I think you didn't believe I could make a success of this place. I think you didn't trust me to find my own bread supplier."

"Not true," he protested, but she ignored him.

"You didn't have faith in my ability, Sam. You don't think I can run this bakery on my own. You think I'll fail without my parents' help, and that's why you interfered." She stared into his melting brown eyes, daring him to deny it. "That's the real truth. Isn't it?"

"No." He straightened and looked her in the eye. "I do believe in you, Joy. I think you've done amazing things with this place. That's why I've celebrated every one of your accomplishments. I *want* you to succeed. I love you."

"Then why...?" She stopped. He sounded so genuine. Was she wrong? No! Because Sam *had* betrayed her.

"I only went to your parents because neither of you were speaking to the other. I thought I could help heal the rift between you," he said firmly. "Because I wanted you to have the kind of family Christmas you always talk about. Because I wanted the very best for you and your kids." His persuasive tone beseeched her to understand. "Because I love you."

His voice trembled on the last words, as if to emphasize his sincerity. But Joy couldn't let Sam's smooth talk soften her. She would not weaken or let him persuade her into forgiveness, not while the same old feelings of being a mistake, of messing up, threatened to overtake her.

"Love isn't dishonest, Sam. Love doesn't go behind the other person's back. Love doesn't humiliate and shame another."

"I would never humiliate you, Joy. I love you."

"It isn't love if it doesn't deal in truth. I think I've learned that lesson well." She pursed her lips. "It starts with lies and prevarication and secrets. Down the road there would be something else to excuse. And then something else after that. I'd always be wondering what you hadn't told me, what else you'd done."

"No, Joy."

"Yes." She swallowed hard. "I put up with all of that during my life with Nick, when he'd disappear with no notice and offer no answers when he returned. But I cannot, I *will not* live like that again. I won't settle for anything less than total honesty between us."

Joy couldn't look at Sam as her fairy-tale world came crashing around her ears. For a little while she'd been blissfully happy. Now she sank into her chair, unable to believe that in a few short hours everything she'd trusted about this man had been a mistake. Once more she'd rushed in too quickly, trusted too easily and had been fooled. Once again, the pain of her rash emotional decision wasn't something she could repair. And once again, the hurt would hang around long after the mistake.

Her fingers gripped the seat of the office chair, which Sam had given her as an opening-day gift, to celebrate her success, he'd said. She glanced at the chair with fresh eyes. Suddenly doubts became questions.

How had he known, without even seeing inside this space, that it was too small to fit a regular office chair, that it could only accommodate one without armrests?

"How did this building just happen to come available just when I needed to move into it?" she whispered as all the inconsistencies she'd noted in the past began to align. "What do you have to do with Possibilities, Sam?"

"Possibilities is a company I formed several years ago so I could buy properties in and around Sunshine. I hoped to refurbish them and hopefully bring in new business or renters." He didn't avoid her stare, didn't hesitate and didn't try to make the truth more palatable.

"You own Possibilities. You're my landlord?" She couldn't make it sink in. "Here as well as the house I rented?" When Sam nodded, she felt as if someone had sucker punched her.

"Dad looks after things for me when I'm on assignment. He's the one who arranged to have the renovations done on this building. I didn't know about it. He said he'd sent me an email explaining, but I was getting so many hate emails after that story that I didn't read most of my inbox."

"And?" She had to hear it all now.

"He'd already contacted the lawyer before I got home, agreeing to rent to you. The first I knew about it was when you got the letter. But I supported his decision completely because *I knew you'd make this place a success.*"

Joy struggled to process his words. So, it wasn't her strength or courage or capability that made her bakery a success. It was Sam.

"I can't believe you told me so many lies," she whispered.

"Not lies, Joy. Never." Sam seemed to know what was coming because he said, "Ask me anything you want."

"Those streetlights that some donor paid to have rewired." She bit her lip. "That was you?"

"Yes, but please don't tell anyone," he said quietly.

"More secrets." Joy heard the snide tone in her own voice and regretted it, but the feeling she'd been duped by the person she'd most trusted had turned her world upside down and she couldn't get a grip.

"Yes, secrets, in this case. You heard how Evan and his buddies are. If they knew I'd paid for those lights, they'd insinuate all kinds of untrue motivations." He shrugged. "I don't want or need the notoriety right now. I just want Sunshine to prosper and do well, to support the people who live here. I want to keep the community alive."

"But—why?" she asked, unable to believe in his altruism.

"I grew up around here, Joy. I've seen little communities around Sunshine fail, mostly because their citizens don't support their own towns and the businesses in them. It's not specific to here. I've seen the same thing all over the world."

"But that's just part of the—" She searched for the right words. "Global trend. Isn't it?"

"You mean the trend for rural folks to order online for the sheer novelty of having something delivered without having to leave their easy chairs? Or the trend for them to travel to the cities to buy because they think they get a better deal?"

"Yes."

"Sadly, I guess it is," he agreed with a nod. "Though I believe it's based on a fallacy. Here's the issue. Taking your commerce away from the place you live is the beginning of a breakdown for smaller towns. If we stop endorsing each other, if we stop buying from our friends and neighbors, if we won't make the effort to support where we live, how can towns like Sunshine, our homes, survive?"

"I guess that's the way of the future," she said, hating the sound of it.

"Maybe, but it doesn't *have* to be like that, Joy." Sam leaned forward in his eagerness. "Look at the people who have flocked to Sunshine. We're not that different from any other town. But we offered something different with Experience Christmas, something unique, something folks want. At its very basic sense, we offered community."

"Why does it matter so much to you, Sam?" Joy couldn't understand his underlying passion. What motivated Sam to go above and beyond when, even after he'd proven himself, some of the people in Sunshine still berated him?

"For me it started years ago when we Calhoun boys came to Sunshine. We were orphaned, injured, with our lives in fragments. Folks in this town went out of their way to make us feel that we fit in, that we were an important part of their world." He smiled. "It didn't matter that Ben and Bonnie adopted us. To Sunshiners we were local kids, one of the gang, and they offered us the same as their own kids. They supported us, believed in us and cheered us on. They needed us. And we needed them."

"But that was then." Joy so wished she'd known Sam when he was a kid. "Things are different now."

"Not for me." Sam shrugged. "When I left Sunshine, I decided that no matter where I went, I'd find a way to invest myself, my money and whatever time I could give to make sure other kids who lived in Sunshine had a chance to experience the same values, the same support, the same feeling of being needed that my brothers and I had." He smiled at her, that amazing, flashing, fascinating smile.

"It's a nice thought but…" She let her words fade away.

"It's more than that. It's important. We all need connections. It really does take a village to raise a child, Joy. The village provides roots, a background, a history. I have a past that has a place in my life and affects my future, all because I lived in Sunshine." He peered straight at her, his voice soft, compelling. "I've traveled around the world, but I never really had a home base, except for Sunshine. This is my home. I want it to succeed and prosper."

"Okay, but what about Evan?"

"Evan and his cronies are a few bruised apples in a town of more than three thousand. Their kind are everywhere, soured on life and needing a scapegoat. They're hurting and so they lash out." He smiled. "They'll get over it eventually. Folks in Sunshine won't let them hang on to their sour grapes. But for now they're disconnected. Our job as their friends and neighbors is to find a way to reconnect them with Sunshine and make them part of it."

"I doubt they want to be part of anything good," she muttered with a frown. "But why not just tell them the truth about what you did?" She didn't get it. "Why not be honest?"

"Do you think Evan cares about honesty?" Sam demanded. "He'd say I was trying to buy their good opinion, to buy back my honesty or something worse." He shook his head emphatically. "I don't want the focus on me. I want the focus to be on Experience Christmas, on how Sunshine, its attitude and its community, can help folks recapture the goodwill toward men that is so hard to come by in this world."

"So those costumes the high school kids needed for their play..." Joy remembered how concerned the kids were about that, and how the next day, the problem had been inexplicably solved. "Did you—"

"When the rental company found out about Experience Christmas, they decided to up the price the kids had negotiated." Sam shrugged. "That wasn't right, so I got a friend of mine to call them and say they were investigating how the company was taking advantage of a town's bad circumstances."

"Adina," she guessed. "The one who's covering the Rose Bowl Parade."

"No comment." Sam inclined his head. "What else do you need to know, Joy? Ask me."

This was her opportunity. She didn't want to hurt him, but she needed to know that everything about Sam wasn't a lie.

"That story," she said slowly. "The report that was false." When Sam hesitated, she reminded him, "You said you'd tell me the truth, but you won't tell me the truth about that?"

"I can tell you part of it," he said very quietly. "But I can't tell you everything because that story is still in play."

"What does that mean?" she asked, confused.

"It means I'll trust you with part of it if you'll believe me when I say that I'm praying everything will be resolved soon. Hopefully by Christmas." He sighed at her dubious expression. "I'm not playing games, Joy. I am deadly serious about this."

"Tell me what you can." She decided to withhold her judgment until she'd heard his explanation.

"I'll have to go back a bit. Excuse me if I stumble or stutter. It's not pretty." Sam heaved a sigh, leaned against the filing cabinet, and began speaking, his voice quiet, even a bit hoarse. "I told you I entered a country illegally to follow up on a report I'd received about its president."

"And you were captured, imprisoned and probably tortured," she said and nodded. "Now you have PTSD. Go on."

"Actually, it's not quite that simple. My captors demanded to know the name of my source. That's where the torture came in. I was pretty sure that if they got a name, they'd kill my source." His voice choked off and then resumed in a bleaker tone. "That's why I couldn't give in to them no matter what they did to me. At all costs I had to protect my source. That irritated them a great deal."

"I can imagine," she said grimly.

"So a few days later my captors threw me in a hole in the desert and left me there. Nobody knew where I was, Joy. Nobody knew that I'd been captured, that I couldn't leave. Not my boss, not my embassy and not my friends. Not even my source. I was all alone, in pain and certain I'd never again be free."

The haunting emptiness of his whispered confession expressed Sam's state of mind better than any other words he could have used.

"You don't have to tell me any more. Don't go through it all again," Joy whispered.

"I need you to understand." Sam inhaled. Several seconds passed before he spoke again. "I don't know how many days passed before they returned. I had no water, no food and the heat was grueling. I was delirious part of the time, unconscious and daydreaming." His face had drained of all color. His hands fisted at his sides as he closed his eyes on the memories.

"Sam, stop."

"I have never felt so alone," he said raggedly. "I felt God had abandoned me. That everyone had. I can't explain the void that was my soul."

"I'm so sorry." Joy wanted to tell him to let it go, but then she realized he might need to speak of it, to finally cleanse the horror that he'd obviously kept bottled inside.

"They must have pulled me out of the hole, because when I came to, I was in some kind of underground room, tied to a chair. When I again refused to talk, they waterboarded me." Agony filled every word. "They shot off guns near my head, which I guess is why loud sounds send me back there."

"Sam—"

"Don't stop me, Joy." He stared at her as the words poured out of him. "They beat me over and over with fists, hands, sticks. I don't even remember all the ways. They used isolation tactics, left the lights on twenty-four hours, played hard rock at loud volume, kept repeating that nobody cared about me, that I was a dead man. Stuff like that. Half the time I was out of it. The only way I knew I hadn't given in to them was because they kept at it. Day after day. For three weeks."

"Until?" she whispered, horrified and feeling ill.

"Until the president himself appeared. He called me a hundred names, spit on me and ordered another beating. But they never touched my face when they beat me."

"Oh. That's strange, isn't it?" she mused.

"I wondered why, too, until he suddenly offered me a deal. I could go free if I reported one last story exactly as they had written it. Any attempt to change the wording or give an impression that it wasn't accurate would result in my death." Sam laughed but it was a miserable cackle. "You know, I actually welcomed that thought, that I could just be done with it. Except I knew I wasn't right with God."

Sam shuddered. His hands shook and his eyes roved back and forth, as if he was trying to erase the memories.

"So you read the story they'd written verbatim. That's the one that the world heard, the untrue one, the one that discredited you."

"Yes." Sam smiled but there was no joy in the curve of his lips. "They waited just long enough for that story to go global, then released information to prove the story was untrue so that anything I reported after wouldn't be believed. The information I'd collected was useless."

"Oh, Sam," she whispered. "All your work and suffering…"

"For nothing." He nodded sadly. "Later, when my vilification was in full swing and I was partially healed, they released me. I had no defense. There was nothing I could do."

"You could have told the world," Joy sputtered. "You didn't bother to offer any explanation at all!"

"No." He stared at her impassively. Silence yawned. It was as if he was trying to tell her something without words. But what?

"Because you couldn't," she whispered, suddenly seeing the truth. Sam always had a reason for his actions. She sorted it out in her mind. "Because there was something—no, someone else in the mix. Because to say anything would be to risk their life?"

He neither confirmed nor denied it.

"Sam?" Joy was so confused, she couldn't make head

or tails of her thoughts. Sam hadn't told her the truth. Sam hadn't told the world the truth. Because...

"In my job—" His voice trembled. He paused, inhaled and began again. "Ever since I've been able to choose my own subjects to cover, I've tried to report on people, places and events in ways that would better the world, wake up its citizens, help us be more responsive to others' plights." He gulped. "But despite my motives, I've ended up hurting people."

"Meaning?" Joy needed all the information she could get. Maybe that would help clear up her misperceptions about this man and what he'd done.

"I did a story on a doctor in Syria once, about how he found needed supplies so he could treat the wounded." Sam closed his eyes. "Somehow someone figured out how he got those supplies and cut them off. Then they killed that doctor. He'd be alive and so would more of his patients if I hadn't told his story."

"But that's not your fault!" she exclaimed.

"There was this family in Brazil with a very bright daughter. A math genius, far above her age and grade level. I featured her in a story." His voice had gone dull now, as if he were reciting tedious facts. "A month after the story aired, the parents lost custody. The girl was taken away from them."

"Why?"

"Recruited to work on some government project? Top secret maybe? I could never find out for sure. I only know I broke up that family, Joy." Regret laced his words. "And then there was Celia. She also died because of me."

"No," Joy interrupted, "she died because someone kidnapped her and didn't provide her inhaler."

"But they kidnapped her because I was too focused on the story, too focused on the crook, on making him pay. And on getting my peers' approval for my work. But Celia's the one who paid—with her life."

"I'm sorry." There was nothing else she could say.

"I loved Celia, Joy." Sam's words were quiet, controlled. "Her death forced me into awareness of how many problems my thoughtless actions and total dedication to my job could cause. I never again wanted anyone to be hurt because of what I said. Her death left a huge hole in me. I was afraid to love again, in case I got hurt again. I've held on to that fear for a long time."

Sam lifted his head to look directly at her. Joy shifted under the intensity of his regard, afraid to hear what he'd say next and yet needing a very strong reason to forget his betrayal, to rebuild her shattered trust in him.

"I never let myself even consider love again," he murmured. "Until you came along with your alligator hat and three special kids."

She had to smile at the memory.

"When you talked about learning trust, I began to realize that trust in God was what I lacked. My faith failed me in that hole because I lost sight of God. I didn't trust He would get me out or help me endure if I had to. In that place, I finally realized just how weak I was without God."

"Oh, Sam." Her heart broke for this generous man and what he'd suffered.

"I didn't know how to change until I came home and my dad and I started studying the Bible. Not until you taught me how to trust, Joy." A wry smile flickered across Sam's lips. "That's one reason I love you so much."

"But Sam." Joy stopped.

How could she explain that despite all he'd said, she couldn't see a way to break free of this horrible feeling of betrayal? She surely didn't feel like she could trust Sam. Or God, for that matter.

She'd trusted Him to take care of her. Why hadn't He spared her this?

"Do you know why I called my company Possibilities?" he asked.

She shook her head.

"Because I wanted to use it to help people see what could be, instead of what is." Sam reached out and tucked a curl behind her ear. "You and your bakery are the best possible demonstration of possibilities. You saw what could be and you charged in to make it happen. Same with the town festival." He smiled. "That's another reason I fell in love with you, Joy."

"But all this time, all the secrets? All the half-truths," she whispered. "You involved my kids. Josh might have recognized my parents' bakery—"

"He did." Sam nodded. "I asked him not to rat me out."

"That's why he was angry at you." She shook her head, ignoring that, for now. "But still, you didn't trust me. Without trust, there isn't love."

"I know that now. And I'm truly sorry, Joy. I only ever wanted the best for you. I never wanted to hurt you."

She couldn't say anything.

"Will you forgive me?" Sam asked in a hushed tone. "Will you give me a second chance?"

"I don't know if I can." She yearned for his embrace, his love, and yet was afraid she'd make another mistake, one she'd regret for the rest of her life. "I need time to sort it all out."

"Take all the time you need, my darling. I'll still be here, waiting." He brushed his fingertip against her lips and peered into her eyes. "But be certain of one thing, Joy. No matter what it seems like, how I acted or what people say, I do love you. More than I ever imagined possible. I'm trusting God to bring you back to me."

Sam's lips touched hers for a fraction of a second and then he was gone.

Joy stood in her office, trying and failing to put the pieces together, to figure out how she could love Sam knowing he'd gone behind her back.

Yes, his motives were probably good, but—

Enough! She couldn't do this now. She had work to do, the day to prepare for. She'd think about it later, when she was alone, when she could let the painful tears flow.

When she could ask God why He'd let her be betrayed, again.

Sam wanted to hide, to nurse his aching heart away from prying eyes.

But the festival was busier than ever now that they'd entered the last week before Christmas. Truthfully, keeping busy helped him forget, even if only for a few minutes, that pained, hurt look in Joy's eyes when he'd finally confessed.

So when Sam had to pick up a pie order for a contest on Monday, he smiled at her as if nothing was wrong. That evening, when she and the kids joined in the family sledding night, he made it a point to engage the kids and pretend nothing had changed.

But it had.

And Miss Partridge, for one, knew it.

"I haven't seen you and Joy together lately, Sam. Is something wrong?" she asked the next morning, after they'd filmed a new video inviting folks to the Christmas Eve potluck.

Sam told her the truth. Not about the Middle East

story, because he hadn't received a new text yet. But he did tell her about his dishonesty.

"I ruined everything by contacting her parents without telling her," he confessed.

"No, you didn't," Grace insisted, pouring him a strong cup of coffee. "You were going where your heart led. That was kind and generous and wonderful."

"You don't seem surprised about my company, Possibilities," he said, suddenly aware that she hadn't voiced the slightest wonder at his revelation.

"My dear, I've known about Possibilities for ages. I researched your incorporation papers years ago. I was a librarian, Sam." She shrugged at his look of disbelief. "You've done good things with that company, just as you have for our town."

"I wish Joy thought that way," he muttered.

"I know Joy wants her relationship with her parents restored," the lady insisted. "I'm just not sure how we could make that happen. Or even if we should. There are so many ways it could go wrong, but so many reasons why success would be worth it," she added with a laugh. "Let's ask for guidance."

Grace began praying, asking God to help them reconcile Joy's family. When she was finished, she lifted her head and looked at him.

"I have no new thoughts, dear," she said. "Perhaps the Lord wants us to wait."

"Yeah, maybe, though I had an idea a while ago." Sam shook his head at her inquiring look. "It involved meddling and I'm not going there again. I need Joy to trust me. That won't happen if she thinks I'm going behind her back to her parents like I did before."

"Just tell *me* the idea and let me mull it over," Grace ordered.

"You don't have time. I know about those two extra projects you've taken on." Sam frowned. "It's too much for…"

"For someone my age?" She shot him a curious look. "I'm fifty-two, Sam. Not quite a fossil."

"Sorry." *Insensitive clod*, his brain accused.

"I've never been trendy. My parents were old fashioned, and I guess they raised me the same." She shrugged. "But however old I grow to be, as long as God gives me strength, I intend to keep helping my friends however I can, and Joy is my dear friend. So what was your idea, Sam?" She leaned forward, her silver-gray hair glinting in the overhead light.

"It was the afternoon we did that practice run for the kids to make their Christmas gifts. Remember? When Trent showed up?" He waited for her nod. "Well, Mom said something about kids' gifts to their parents and how nobody could resist a kid's handmade gift. How it melted your heart."

"And?" Grace frowned at him. "That's why we organized it in the first place, Sam."

"I know. So what if Joy's parents got handmade gifts from their own grandchildren? On Christmas Eve," he added. Then he shook his head. "It's still meddling, still going behind her back."

"Which *you* are definitely not going to do." Grace gathered her notes and plopped her knitted purple cloche on her head. "I have to go. I'm to man the hot chocolate booth for an hour. Mona Blanchet wants to go skating with her grandson."

"What?" Sam did a double take and stared at her. "But she's—"

"In a wheelchair. I know." Grace buttoned her coat and drew on her gloves, a funny smile teasing her lips. "He's going to push her over the ice. She can hardly wait. She said you gave her the idea." She leaned over and hugged him, her lilac fragrance enveloping him. "I could kiss you, Sam, for bringing such joy and love to Sunshine. You are a blessing. Gotta go. Bye."

With a wave, she was out the door.

"If I bring such love, why can't Joy love me?" With no answer to his question, Sam sighed wearily, got to his feet and studied his list. *Check that all the props for the live nativity walk-through are in place.*

He headed for the acres behind the church where the walk would be held.

"This is just a glitch," he murmured, praying as he walked. "Joy will love me again. I'm trusting You."

But saying the words wasn't the same as believing them.

Chapter Thirteen

They'd called it *Bethlehem Live*.

"Isn't it wonderful, Mom?" Josh hadn't said a word until they'd moved through the entire series of picturesque scenes, past the live actors who recited parts of the story of Jesus's birth. "Ben and I helped make some of the props."

"They're very good," she said automatically, wondering if she'd see Sam tonight.

"How did they get the angel who talked to Mary get up so high?" Cris wondered.

"I liked all the sheep with those shepewds," Becca murmured, awed by what they'd seen and heard. "They had lots and lots of angels singing. What did you like best, Mommy?"

"I liked the baby Jesus lying in the manger with his mom and dad right there," Joy told her, amazed that the little family scene had awakened so much longing in her.

"The cows just stood there." Josh shook his head. "I don't know how they got them to stay still. It was great."

"I liked the stowies that they said at each place. Just like we wed in the Bible last night." Becca clung to Joy's hand, shuffling through the snow as they followed others into the church hall for warm cider and cookies. "Did you make all these cookies, Mommy?"

"No, just some of them. The ones shaped like bells with red bows on them," she said before her kids could ask which were hers.

As they filed through the food line, Joy noticed Sam standing to one side, his eyes on her as he listened to something the mayor was saying. Sam didn't seem to like whatever he was hearing, because he frowned and shook his head. When he shifted as if to move away, the mayor clasped his arm and kept talking.

"We hafta move, Mom." Josh nudged her back to awareness, indicating the gap in the line in front of them.

"Sorry." She waited at the serving bar while they chose their cookies. Then Grace appeared and offered to carry Becca's and Cris's drinks. "I haven't seen you for a bit," she said with a smile. "What have you been up to?"

"Oh, this and that." Grace waved an airy hand. "Hello, children. How are you? Got your Christmas gifts all ready?"

"Uh-huh. We just have to pick them up." Josh avoided Joy's glance.

"What gifts?' she asked. The guilty looks on her children's faces unnerved her until Grace fluttered a hand.

"My dear, you know that one never discusses secrets before Christmas," she scolded with a chuckle. "Now, children, since tomorrow is Christmas Eve, I'm going to need your help. Is that all right, Joy?'

"I suppose." She opened her mouth to ask why, but Grace shook her head and set her forefinger against her lips. Sighing, Joy shrugged. "You'll bring them to me at the bakery when your secret mission is over?"

"Of course. Now I must get back to my station." She

paused when Joy cleared her throat. "Was there something else, dear?"

"I wondered whose idea it was to have a food drive tonight instead of charging admission." Joy grimaced. "Not that it's any of my business, but won't the people who want to enter the grand-prize draw be upset?"

"I don't know why," Grace said. "They can still enter if they attend Bethlehem Live tonight. The only difference is they pay with a food donation. Sam suggested that since we'd met our goal for the hall and more besides, we might gather food to be given to those who need it so they, too, can *experience* Christmas." She grinned. "The committee thought that was a fantastic idea."

"So do I." Joy reached into her purse. "I didn't have time to go to the store, so I made out these gift certificates. They can either be given directly to the families or used to purchase items from the bakery for a food hamper."

"Joy, that's lovely. Thank you." Grace tucked the envelopes into her pocket, leaned over to hug Joy and then hurried away, her face beaming.

"Hi, guys."

Joy startled, unaware that Sam had come up behind them. She waited until the kids had greeted him and exclaimed over what they'd seen.

"How long will *Bethlehem Live* operate?" she wondered, trying to repress a tiny thrill at his proximity.

"Tonight and tomorrow night, Christmas Eve. Then it comes down," he said. "How are you, Joy?"

"Oh, I'm fine. Busy, but that's good." She couldn't look at him, so she gathered her things, preparing to leave. "Finish up, children. I have some things to do at home tonight."

"Well, I'll let you get to them." The sad look in his

eyes, despite his smile, hurt to see. His whispered "I miss you, Joy" broke through all her defenses.

She wanted to tell Sam she forgave him. She wanted that so badly. But that feeling of being in the dark, of having someone go behind her back—that was what she couldn't get past.

"I guess we'll see you at the potluck tomorrow evening. It's hard to believe Christmas is almost here, isn't it?" she said, trying to infuse joy into her voice. "You've accomplished so much in such a short time. You should be very proud, Sam."

"Should I?" He simply watched her, his expression empty.

Joy had never seen Sam like this, with no animation, no expression. With his sparkling brown eyes vacant and empty. Yet something inside her felt tied down, held back by anger and sad memories of the past. It wouldn't let her break free.

"Let's go, kids. Someone else is waiting for our place here." Joy rose and turned to say goodbye to Sam, but he was bent over, his ear next to Becca's lips, listening.

"They're not open now," he said after glancing at his watch. "But Miss Partridge says you're helping her tomorrow. I think you can pick up your parcel then. Okay?"

"Thank you, Sam." Becca wrapped her chubby arms around his neck, squeezed her eyes closed and hugged him as if he was the most precious person in her world.

Joy's eyes filled at the look that swam over Sam's face as he brushed a kiss against her daughter's curly hair and patted her cheek.

"See you tomorrow, sweetheart." He turned to face Cris, who thrust out his hand as if he was afraid Sam would hug him, too. "See you, Cris."

"Yeah." Her son's face wrinkled with a frown. "Do

you think—" He stopped, looked at Joy then licked his lips. "Um…"

"I think we've done all we can, Cris. It's up to God now." Before Joy could ask any questions, Sam nodded at Josh then walked away.

"Sam's so cool," Josh said as they walked out to the van. "I want to be just like him."

Though surprised at his about-face, Joy agreed with her son.

Sam truly was a man to admire. Except— *Stop thinking about Sam!*

"Can we deliver our Christmas presents tomorrow before the church service?" Josh asked as they rode home.

"How many gifts do you have?" Joy inquired curiously.

"Lots. Sam helped us."

"He did? How?" Joy wondered how she'd managed to miss it.

"Sam helped us earn money. We all got jobs so we could get things. Or we made things. Sam says Christmas is all about giving." Cris sighed. "Sam's great."

"Yeah, he is. We had so much fun doing stuff, even secret stuff that nobody knows about." Josh laughed with delight.

"Like what?" Joy asked, half-afraid to hear the answer.

"It's secwet, Mommy!" Becca's voice held a reprimand.

"Don't worry. It was all good stuff." Josh's voice sobered. "Sam has a way of seeing things, like noticing stuff nobody else does. He helped us look so we could see it, too. This has been the best Christmas ever."

"An' Christmas isn't even here yet!" Cris exclaimed.

Joy should have been smiling. She'd wanted her children to have a wonderful Christmas. That was why she'd worked so hard to make things good for them, and yet it was Sam who'd taught her children that joy came from giving, and that the joy was even greater when no one knew what you'd done.

She was so confused. She thought she loved Sam. She certainly wanted to spend Christmas with him, wanted to feel the same joy and excitement that her children did. But…

As she pulled into the yard, in front of the log house where Sam had brought them a little less than a month ago, Joy felt torn in ten directions. She'd made so many mistakes. She couldn't afford another. And yet, it felt like not grabbing on to the love Sam offered was also a mistake.

But how could she love him if she couldn't trust him?

"Please tell me what to do," she prayed later that night, when no one but God could hear.

If God answered, she didn't hear Him.

All she heard was her father saying, *He insisted we had to let you sell our bread or your bakery would fail.*

Christmas Eve Day, and Sam was killing time.

Most everything was finished. The last of the events were happening as planned. There wasn't much more for him to do. And still his burner phone remained silent.

God knows your heart, son. Just keep trusting Him to work it all out. Ben's advice returned full force as Sam entered the town offices and came face-to-face with his nemesis.

"Merry Christmas, Evan."

"Think you're pretty clever, don't you? That you've pulled the wool over our eyes with all the shenanigans you've created in Sunshine? But the truth is coming out now, boy." That sneer sent Sam's temperature rising, but he refused to show it.

"What truth is that?" he asked, noticing that several men were gathering around them.

"The one about that lie you told when you were in the Middle East. I just read online that your chum Adelia intends to reveal the whole story about your lies, for all the world to hear."

"Really?" Sam clung to his composure. "Well, you'll be sure to watch, won't you?" He had to get out of here, but as he eased past Evan, the man spoke again.

"Don't know what you're going to do with all the food that's coming into the hall, Sam." Something in his words made Sam falter.

"Eat it?" Sam's guard went up. The snide smiles shared between these men told him evil was afoot.

"Won't be that many there to eat it. We're asking folks to boycott the potluck. We want the truth from you and we're going to have it. And you can forget about council hiring you."

"Hiring me? Are you sick, Evan?" Sam didn't like being in the dark. "Why don't you get over yourself and just enjoy Christmas? Or if you can't do that, at least let other people enjoy it. Make merry and all that. You know?"

"I'll do that, buddy, when you come groveling to this town on your hands and knees, asking for forgiveness." Evan and his band muscled their way out of the room.

That was when Sam saw Grace, standing at the end of the hall, her rigid posture perfectly expressing her fury.

"I would like to shake that man until sense flows into his empty head," she snapped.

"He was talking about council hiring me." Something flickered across her face. "What's going on, Grace?"

"I can't talk about it right now. Nothing for you to worry about, I assure you." She was tugging on her coat as she spoke. "I need to get reinforcements."

"Because?" Sam stood directly in front of her.

"Because those men are holding a meeting in about five minutes to persuade some town councilors not to offer you the job of economic development officer that we'd voted on doing at the last meeting." She slapped her beret on her head. "They're also going to request you be asked to leave Sunshine. But they don't run the entire town. Not yet. Excuse me, dear."

She rushed away before he could ask her anything else.

Economic development officer? Sam smiled. He'd like that, a full-time job figuring out ways to make Sunshine better.

Then his smile faded. But Evan would ruin it. If only the text he'd been waiting for would arrive. If only he could finally clear his name.

"What is taking so long, Lord? I'm trying to trust, but—no, I *will* trust."

Sam zipped up his jacket and went to find Joy's kids. Grace had probably forgotten they'd need to pick up their gifts. He'd see to it. Maybe he'd even get a chance to talk to Joy.

His burner phone vibrated against his chest.

Sam caught his breath, squeezed his eyes closed and breathed, "God?"

"Evan is doing *what*?" Joy gaped at her friend.

"He's calling a meeting to discuss running Sam out of town," Grace repeated.

"Can he do such a thing?"

"Technically, no. But he can make it very miserable for Sam. I'm worried," she admitted. "Those men have grown mean and so bitter with their hate. Now they're trying to draw others in, and some, particularly those retail folks who never got on the bandwagon with Experience Christmas, have just enough sourness to listen to Evan."

"Well, it's sad, but it's not any of my business. I'm the newcomer. I have my own issues," Joy protested.

"You're part of this town, dear. And such animosity hurts everyone," Grace protested sternly. "I've argued long and hard, but no one will listen to me anymore. It's going to take a fresh voice. You have to help. If you're not part of the solution, you're part of the problem, Joy. Sam needs you now more than ever. He stood up for you."

He'd also shown her kids how to really live Christmas every day. God had brought him to Sunshine for a reason. And this was a matter of trust. Would she give or withhold it?

The truth smacked Joy head-on. She'd held on to her anger and her betrayed feelings just like Evan. She'd refused to trust that God would heal her heart. Refused to believe Sam, too.

Because she was afraid.

But God was in charge. Not Evan Smith. Not even Sam.

"God works through people, dear," her friend chided her very quietly. "He could work through you if you make yourself available."

Joy made one of her split-second decisions. But she knew she would never regret this one.

"I gave Honey the afternoon off. I'll have to lock up, even though I've got a bunch of fudge orders some kids are supposed to pick up," Joy said, mentally reorganizing her work. "Guess I'll have to deliver them."

"Don't be silly. I'll stay here. I might even sell out

what's left." Miss Partridge grinned. "Go on, dear. Go tell them the truth. I'll be right here, praying for you."

"You're sure—"

"I'm positive," Grace insisted. "He is far greater than we can even ask or think, dear. Trust Him."

There were so many people in town and so much traffic that Joy decided it would be quicker to go on foot. She half ran through the streets, hoping she wouldn't be too late. She pushed open the door and walked into the community hall, where angry words and accusations against Sam spilled like raindrops.

I can do this, she prayed silently. *With Your help.*

"What do you want here?" Evan Smith demanded. "You were not invited to this meeting."

"Why wasn't I?" Joy calmly slid her coat from her shoulders and placed it on an empty chair.

"Because you're a friend of Sam's."

Joy couldn't help it. She started laughing and couldn't stop.

A friend of Sam's? Yes, indeed.

And so much more, Lord, if You can manage it.

Chapter Fourteen

Startled by the number of cars still gathered around the community hall when he knew there were no event scheduled there until the potluck tonight, Sam decided the *run-me-out-of-town* meeting scheduled for earlier must still be going on. Taking a deep breath, he went to investigate.

He stepped through the side door, but at the sound of Evan's voice he wheeled around, prepared to get out and avoid another confrontation. Until he heard Joy.

"I must say, I don't understand your attitude, Mr. Smith," she said.

Sam edged his head around the corner and just managed to catch a glimpse of her, covered in her bakery whites, slim and defiant as she addressed the former mayor.

"You're like a bear with a sore paw, Evan. You won't let anyone fix it and you won't do anything to help yourself. Instead you go around picking on those around you, making their lives miserable so they can join in your misery."

Muffled snickers filled the room. Sam couldn't suppress his own grin.

"You list grievance after grievance, but you never list anything kind or good, even though your burger stand has profited a lot from Experience Christmas. Most evenings and weekends your place is packed. You've benefitted from the other events Sam planned, too, and from the work everyone in town has put into making the festival work. Everyone, that is, but you." Sam peeked again and saw her studying Evan, hands on her hips. "When do you ever contribute to this town? Or do you just keep taking?"

"Now, just a minute!"

"No. I am going to have my say because I'm sick and tired of the undercurrents you cause in our town. Your animosity is hurting everyone in Sunshine. It's time it stopped."

No one spoke; no one told Joy to sit down or be quiet. Sam had a hunch the fire in her words matched the fire in her eyes. He'd never been prouder.

"Sam came home to Sunshine, probably to rest and relax with his family and friends after a grueling time in the Middle East. He didn't ask you for anything. He didn't even ask you to put up funds to repair the community hall that all of *you* have neglected for years."

"He told us to take out a loan," Evan blustered.

"Which he backed from his own pocket. Did I miss hearing you offer to chip in, Mr. Smith?" Joy paused only a second. "Then Sam got to work planning, conceiving and carrying out the finest event this town has ever seen. He never asked you to pay him. He never argued when you wouldn't agree to his suggestions. Sam simply got on with trying to make this town, *our* town, better."

Sam could hardly believe what he was hearing. Joy was defending him. As if she cared about him.

"Sam only did it to win approval," one of Evan's supporters called out.

"Really?" Joy turned on him in a flash. "One wonders why Sam, an award-winning journalist with years of reporting hard-hitting stories from some of the most neglected places on this earth, should need *your* approval, sir?"

Sam wanted to tell her to stop, but he couldn't speak. He was too fascinated by Joy's defense to interrupt. Besides, he wanted to hear more. Maybe then he'd be able to tell if she really, truly did love him.

"What about that last story?" Evan said, a sneer on his face.

"Yes, let's talk about *that* story," Joy said pleasantly, moving to stand directly in front of the disagreeable man. "I'm guessing you didn't know, maybe because you didn't ask, that Sam was trying to ascertain the truth of information he'd received about a crooked official. So you also probably didn't know that he was captured, held against his will, without his embassy, his employer or anyone else knowing because he was kept in isolation."

"How do *you* know that's true?" someone called.

"Because Sam told me and I believe him. Why would he make it up?" She gave Evan a scornful look then moved to the front. "But you didn't ask. So you certainly wouldn't know why Sam was forced to file that false story. Of course he knew it was false, as would any journalist who has been around as much as Sam would know, so it follows that he must have also known that releasing it would cost him all credibility. *But that didn't stop him*," she whispered, the words clearly carrying in the now-silent room.

Joy was a natural at public speaking, Sam decided. Or perhaps she was too engaged in what she was saying to realize she held the crowd in the palm of her hand.

"But why didn't he?" Evan asked in a quieter tone. "Why would he let it stand?"

"Why indeed? For some higher good? Maybe. Or perhaps he did it because he's Sam," Joy told him with a smile. "Because there were issues at stake which he deemed more important than his own career. Because he has integrity."

Nobody said anything. Everyone was staring at Joy.

"Don't you get it even yet?" she asked, her voice louder, angrier. "Why did Sam come to Sunshine and do all he's done for you and for me, and for the many people who've come here to celebrate the meaning of Christmas?"

"You're going to tell us," Evan snapped.

"Someone needs to," Joy replied scathingly. "You obviously can't understand that Sam doesn't need your approval in the least. But he does deserve your respect for trying to make the world he inhabits a better place. What are *you* doing about that?"

Applause started in one corner of the room and grew as those clapping rose to their feet and yelled, "Bravo, Joy!"

She blinked, obviously startled. Her head swiveled to stare at those who remained in their seats, unwilling or unable to understand what Christmas was about. She flushed a deep, dark red before she grabbed her coat and headed for the door. That was when Sam stepped out of his hiding place and stood directly in her path.

"Oh," she whispered, her green eyes huge, her crisp strawberry blond curls bouncing at her abrupt stop. "Hi."

"Hi, yourself. Thank you, Joy," he said, for her ears alone.

He wasn't sure why she kept staring at him or what she intended. All Sam knew was that she grabbed his hand in hers and clung to it like a lifeline while she faced the room.

"This is the man I'm going to marry," she announced very clearly. "If that means you don't want us here, that you want us to leave Sunshine, we will. But it will be your loss because Sam has great plans for next year. So do I."

A second later Joy was kissing him. It took Sam a second before he kissed her back, right in front of everyone. She drew back too soon.

"I have to get my kids," she told him, still red-faced, but now smiling.

"Then let's go." He took her hand and rushed outside with her, skittering through the snow-covered streets like a pair of giddy children to the department store where Sam said he'd left his car so he could pick them up before closing.

Once the children emerged and were settled inside, their gifts secured in the trunk, Joy looked at Sam.

"Do we have time to go home and put their gifts under the tree and for me to change before the potluck?" she asked.

"They want to drop off their gifts at Grace's first," Sam said.

"Oh, no." Joy clapped her hands to her cheeks.

"What's wrong now?" Sam asked wearily, wondering if they'd ever get a moment alone.

"Grace. I left her by herself at the bakery." Joy made a face. "She doesn't have a key to lock up, so she's still stuck there. Come on."

The bakery looked empty. Only a small light on the counter lit up the area. The shelves were completely empty. They found Grace seated at a table, patiently waiting.

"Hello, dears," she said, smiling at their clasped hands. "All better now?"

"I love Joy," Sam said.

"I love Sam," Joy said.

"I know." Grace Partridge checked her watch. "It's time for the potluck."

"I think I have a clean shirt in my office. I'll just take a minute," Joy assured them.

She took a few more, but no one minded. They had to

wait at the community hall anyway. The line for the potluck was very long. Over and over, visitors came to tell Grace how wonderful she was in the ads, how they appreciated her work as the Christmas lady. She, of course, tried to defer to Sam, but he waved off her attempts.

"You deserve it. Enjoy it, Grace," Sam said. "You were the busiest, best coworker I've ever had."

"Thank you, dear. Now I must go. I believe I'm on coffee duty." She left to help out somewhere, because that was what Grace Partridge did. She helped.

"When things settle down, we've really got to find someone for her to fall in love with," he told Joy.

"Yes, we do," she agreed, squeezing his hand under the table.

"By the way," he murmured in her ear, "I've got something to tell you."

Joy smiled as if she knew exactly what that was. "I've got something to tell you, too."

"No, but—" Sam gave up when the pastor rapped the table for silence.

"If you could all help us clear up, we have something important to share. Please gather in the church sanctuary as soon as you are able."

"I need to explain—"

"I love you, too, Sam. But I think we'd better save that for later, until we're alone," Joy told him, her green eyes glowing. "There's something happening here."

"That's what—I was going to tell you," he finished when she hurried away with their soiled dishes. "I wanted the rest of that pie," he said mournfully.

"You're in love with a baker, Sam." Evan stood beside him. "From what I saw, she'll bake you one whenever you want." The other man thrust out his hand. "Merry Christmas, Sam. And my deepest apologies."

"None needed, Evan. Merry Christmas."

* * *

Joy sat in the sanctuary beside Sam, her hand tucked in his. He was happier than he'd ever been.

"Church looks pretty good in its Christmas finery, doesn't it?" he whispered.

"It looks amazing. But I wonder why the screen is down. It blocks out so many of the decorations." Joy frowned as if she wanted to go wind the thing up herself.

After her performance this afternoon, Sam figured she would do it, too. So just to be safe, he tightened his hand around hers and hung on.

"Welcome here tonight," the pastor said, his smile huge. "Before we begin the service, we have two orders of business to take care of. First, we're going to draw the name of the winner of our Experience Christmas festival. As you all know, the prize is a trip to the Rose Bowl Parade and a feature segment with Adelia Forsyth before the parade."

The draw was made by the mayor and everyone clapped for the winner.

"Evan Smith? He had the nerve to put his name in the draw?" Joy couldn't believe it.

"I think it's great." Sam smirked. "He'll have no excuse for not helping us out next year, right?"

"I guess," Joy said, obviously still disgruntled.

"Now to our second order of business," the pastor announced. "Adelia Forsyth has sent us an exclusive partial clip of a newscast that will air in the new year. Let's watch."

Sam put his arm around Joy's shoulders and hugged her against him as Adelia appeared on-screen.

"Join us as we share world-class reporter Sam Calhoun's moving story about a harrowing trek into the Middle East to expose a corrupt president. The only reason we're finally able to hear this story is because Sam's source has now escaped the regime and is safe with his family in an undisclosed location. But I'll let Sam tell you a little about what to expect."

Sam and Adelia had done Sam's hurried interview via Skype right after the burner phone had freed him from his obligations. Adelia's videographer had then impressively amassed archived bits of video from Sam's career for this promo piece. He sat immobile, listening to his own recorded voice explain how he'd verified each point of his informant's claim but was unable to release that story because he'd been captured. For this clip Sam had deliberately downplayed the pain and suffering he'd gone through, not wanting to spoil Christmas Eve.

"I'm truly sorry I reported an untrue story," he heard himself say. "But at the time, I had no other alternative. I could not give my source's name. I could not allow him or his family to be captured and probably killed by such an evil man. Telling that lie was the only way I could gain my own release and keep my friend and his loved ones safe. I am so very glad they are now able to enjoy Christmas together. Though is has been a traumatic time for me, the end result is that what my enemies meant for evil, God meant for good. This is Sam Calhoun reporting from Sunshine, Montana, wishing you a very Merry Christmas."

The clip was short to encourage viewers to tune in to the whole story in the new year. Sam felt nothing but relief when the organ sounded and the candles were passed out so the service could finally begin.

Once, he'd sought the limelight. Now he preferred the privacy his hometown offered.

Together the town celebrated the night of Christ's birth together in a reverent, hallowed service, with peace and calm and joy. Sam felt a oneness with his Lord that he hadn't experienced for years. He could tell by Joy's shining face that she felt the same.

When the ceremony was over, they and the children left as quickly as possible because he and Joy wanted to celebrate their first family Christmas at the ranch. Once again, someone needed to borrow Sam's car, so they all walked to the bakery and rode to Hanging Hearts Ranch in Joy's van.

The mood was festive as the kids teased him about being on television. But the three youngsters were weary from all their labors and went to bed early, in eager anticipation of the next day.

Finally Joy and Sam were alone.

"I don't know how to thank you for what you said in my defense, Joy," he told her, holding her hands in his. "It was an amazing speech. I couldn't believe it. You were awesome."

"Yes, I was," she said and then laughed. "I couldn't believe I did it either, but some sort of righteous indignation just took hold of me and spilled out." She squeezed his hand. "Anyway, I owed you some public recognition. You've been so patient while I fought through the doubts and fears about my mistakes. It took those men and their scheming to make me realize that my trust is just words if I don't act on it." She pressed a kiss against his lips. "I love you, Sam. And I trust you."

"Ditto, Mrs. Baker." He kissed her back, until they were both breathless. Then they sat, arms around each other, content to watch the fire and go over everything once more.

"It's late. I need to go home." But Sam didn't move. Instead he studied her for so long that she shifted under his scrutiny.

"What?" she asked, a frown marring her beauty.

"I'm afraid I may have misunderstood something you said earlier and I'd like to clarify it."

"Okay." She looked wary.

Sam knelt in front of Joy, clinging to her hands

"Darling, Joy. You fill my heart and my soul. I want to be better, do better, work harder with you in my life. I want us to be a family, to be a dad to your kids, if they'll let me. I want to share my family with yours. Will you marry me, Joy?"

"I already told everyone at that meeting that I was marrying you, Sam," she said, blushing furiously.

"I know. I heard. I'm just making sure you haven't changed your mind." Sam grinned at her droll look. "So? Marry me, Joy?"

"Yes," she said simply. "I've spent my whole life waiting for you, even when I didn't know it." They kissed and Joy sighed.

"What?" Sam asked.

"I guess you managed to give me my family Christmas, didn't you?" She kissed him again, but there was a bitter sweetness to it because they both knew her parents wouldn't be part of it.

"Trust, remember?" Sam encouraged softly.

"I am," she said. "I will. Life is going to be so wonderful for us, Sam. I love you."

"I love you, too."

An hour later Sam walked home through the snow, thrilled by how God had come through for them.

"There's just one more little thing, Lord," he murmured as he watched the stars appear. "And I'm trusting You about that, too."

Epilogue

Christmas Morning

"How did you make such a lovely thing, Josh?" Joy turned the handmade rolling pin over and over, amazed by the smooth yet sturdy feel he'd achieved. "It's wonderful and I'll use it forever. Thank you, son."

"Welcome." Josh smiled, endured her hug and then went back to his new video game.

"This is for you, Mommy. From me and Cwis." Becca's grin now boasted a missing front tooth. "We love you."

"I love you, too, you sweethearts. But how—" She turned her head toward Sam and knew instantly that he'd had something to do with it. What a guy!

"Open it," he said quietly.

She parted the delicate tissue paper and caught her breath. A beautiful green satin robe with hand-stitched silver embroidery lay nestled inside.

"It's amazing," she said, rising to model it. "And it fits so perfectly. But how on earth did you get it?"

"We worked," Cris said proudly. "We helped other kids make their Christmas presents and we cleaned up the crafts and we did lots of cutting out decorations for Miss Grace."

"An' I dwad some stuff an' put the ABC's wight, an' lotsa stuff." Becca wasn't to be left out.

"They really earned their money," Sam told her. "They're very good workers."

"Thank you, children. I am so proud of you and all you've done." Joy kissed each of them, refolded her robe and then headed for the kitchen. "I need another cup of coffee."

"Me, too." Sam followed her, his arms curving around her waist as he held her fast. "I have another gift for you, Mrs. Baker."

"But Sam," she argued, turning to face him. "You've already given me so many gifts. And all I gave you was that sweater I knitted."

"Which I love. This is from me to you, Joy." He slid an emerald solitaire ring on her finger. "I asked your kids and they said it's okay if we get married."

"Oh, Sam." Ecstatic, Joy kissed him then wiggled her hand free so she could get a better look. "It's beautiful. Thank you."

"It was my birth mother's. It reminds me of your eyes. I thought it could be the start of one of our traditions. Oof!" he grunted when she threw her arms around him, but he certainly didn't protest when she kissed him so thoroughly that he lost his breath.

Then someone knocked on the door.

"I thought the family sleigh ride was tonight—" Joy pulled open the door and stared. "Mom? Dad? What are you doing here?"

"Merry Christmas, Joy. We came to ask you to forgive us for not being part of your and the children's lives." Her mother was weeping. "The loss has been all ours."

"Blame it on a stubborn old man," her dad stammered. "But we never stopped loving you, Joy. Never."

Joy gave a squeal of delight and flew into their arms. In that instant, all was forgiven.

"Would you like to come inside?" Sam asked with a smile. "It's nice and warm if you close the door. Glad you could make it, by the way."

Her parents entered and closed the door behind them, handing their coats to Sam.

"You knew they were coming?" Joy demanded, frowning at him.

"Nope." Sam shook his head. "I prayed. And I trusted God," he said before inviting everyone to sit down.

"Well, what changed your minds?" Joy asked after she'd introduced her children.

"Their gifts." Her mother dabbed her eyes. "How could any grandmother resist a child's Christmas gift?"

"Your mother said that, too, Sam." Joy studied him suspiciously. "Did you—"

"Grace Partridge," he explained with a grin.

"But Sam helped." Becca hugged him. "He took us to the Fespex."

"The what?" Joy looked to Sam for an explanation, but Cris answered first.

"The Federal Express office," he explained. "Sam said we needed as express as we could get if we were gonna get you a real family Christmas at Hanging Hearts Ranch."

"Will you ever stop trying to surprise me, Sam?" Joy asked later that night when they were alone.

"I hope not, Mrs. Baker. Soon to be Mrs. Baker Calhoun." Sam gazed at his betrothed. "Because I'm constantly surprised that you love me. And I assure you, the feeling is entirely mutual."

"There will be some tough times though," she warned, loving the feeling of his strong arms around her. "So, we have to keep trusting each other completely. And God."

"He's the one who holds our future in His hands. And if I ever forget it," Sam murmured, tilting her chin to stare into her eyes, "you just put on your alligator hat to remind me."

"I love you, Sam." Joy savored the memories of how God had brought them together before asking, "Would you mind if I kissed you again, Sam, just to make sure I'm not dreaming?"

"Bring it, sweetheart," he whispered, right before bent his head and kissed her.

* * * * *

If you enjoyed this story, pick up these other stories from Lois Richer:

A Dad for Her Twins
Rancher Daddy
Gift-Wrapped Family
Accidental Dad
Meant-to-Be Baby
Mistletoe Twins
Rocky Mountain Daddy
Rocky Mountain Memories
Hoping for a Father
Home to Heal

Available now from Love Inspired!

Find more great reads at
www.LoveInspired.com.

Dear Reader,

Welcome back to Hanging Hearts Ranch. I hope you've enjoyed Sam's and Joy's journeys through the hard parts of life to find each other through trusting God. Trust is such a difficult thing to learn, isn't it? Just when you think you've got it down pat, something happens and you're forced to figure it out all over again. Or perhaps that's just me.

I confess to being a Christmas lover. The sights, the sounds, the smiles, the generosity, the curiosity—all of it draws me into remembering God's great love for we unworthy humans who inhabit His creation. He sent His only son! Now that's true love.

I'd love to hear from you, either through Love Inspired, via email at loisricher@gmail.com, or snail mail at Box 639, Nipawin, SK Canada S0E 1E0. Or you can check out my webpage at loisricher.com.

As we celebrate Christmas once more, I wish joy for you, abounding delight that fills your soul so full it gives you strength and courage and stays with you through the entire new year.

Merry Christmas!

Lois
Richer

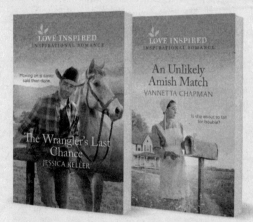

COMING NEXT MONTH FROM
Love Inspired

Available December 29, 2020

AN AMISH WINTER
by Vannetta Chapman and Carrie Lighte
Amish hearts are drawn together in these two sweet winter novellas, where an Amish bachelor rescues a widowed single mother stranded in a snowstorm, and an Amish spinster determined never to marry falls for her friend's brother-in-law when her trip south for the winter is delayed.

THE AMISH BAKER'S RIVAL
by Marie E. Bast
Sparks fly when an *Englischer* opens a store across from Mary Brenneman's bakery. With sales declining, she decides to join a baking contest to drum up business. But she doesn't expect Noah Miller to be her biggest rival—and her greatest joy.

OPENING HER HEART
Rocky Mountain Family • by Deb Kastner
Opening a bed-and-breakfast is Avery Winslow's dream, but she's not the only one eyeing her ideal location. Jake Cutter is determined to buy the land and build a high-end resort. Can his little girl and a sweet service dog convince him and Avery that building a family is more important?

THE RANCHER'S FAMILY SECRET
The Ranchers of Gabriel Bend • by Myra Johnson
Risking his family's disapproval because of a long-standing feud, Spencer Navarro is determined to help his neighbor, Lindsey McClement, when she returns home to save her family ranch. But as they work together, can they keep their forbidden friendship from turning into something more?

A FUTURE FOR HIS TWINS
Widow's Peak Creek • by Susanne Dietze
Tomás Santos and Faith Latham both want to buy the same building in town, and neither is willing to give up the fight. But Tomás's six-year-old twins have plans to bring them together. After all, they want a mom...and they think Faith is the perfect fit!

AN UNEXPECTED ARRANGEMENT
by Heidi McCahan
Jack Tomlinson has every intention of leaving his hometown behind—until twin babies are left on his doorstep. He needs help, and the best nanny he knows is Laramie Chambers. But proving he's not just her best friend's irresponsible brother might be a bigger challenge than suddenly becoming a dad...

LOOK FOR THESE AND OTHER LOVE INSPIRED BOOKS WHEREVER BOOKS ARE SOLD, INCLUDING MOST BOOKSTORES, SUPERMARKETS, DISCOUNT STORES AND DRUGSTORES.

LICNM1220